ATTACK OF THE LONELY HEARTS

WINNER!
39TH ANNUAL
3-DAY NOVEL
WRITING
CONTEST

Attack

of the
Lonely Hearts

by
Mark Wagstaff

Winner of the 39th Annual 3-Day
Novel Writing Contest

ANVIL PRESS • 2017

Copyright © 2017 by Mark Wagstaff

Anvil Press Publishers Inc.
P.O. Box 3008, Main Post Office
Vancouver, B.C. V6B 3X5 CANADA
www.anvilpress.com

Library and Archives Canada Cataloguing in Publication

Wagstaff, Mark, author
     Attack of the lonely hearts / Mark Wagstaff. — 1st edition.

Winner of the 39th Annual 3-Day Novel Contest.
ISBN 978-1-77214-103-0 (paperback)

     I. Title.

PS8607.I213C43 2017   C813'.6   C2017-903991-9

Printed and bound in Canada
Cover design by Derek von Essen
Interior by HeimatHouse
Represented in Canada by Publishers Group Canada
Distributed by Raincoast Books

The publisher gratefully acknowledges the financial assistance of the Canada Council for the Arts, the Canada Book Fund, and the Province of British Columbia through the B.C. Arts Council and the Book Publishing Tax Credit.

'For the dreamers and the dancers'.

To Sam
with thanks for
everything —
then and now!
All good wishes
Mark

12/12/2017

1.

This room has looked so much better. There were flowers on the shelf, though they died and had to get swept up. A comfortable couch with just a spring or two loose. There was the table, where they ate dinner together every night from when they got married 'til a year, or maybe two years after. Anyways, they ate dinner. There were pictures on the wall, candy bright imitations of summer days.

Now look at the place. All the furniture gone, eddies of dust swirled into the corner, a few pages torn from the *Times* crumpled on the floor. Light rectangles on the gray walls where pictures once hung.

Now look at her—okay-looking, maybe, but a mess. Hair stuffed anyhow inside the collar of a coat that has seen three more winters than its makers intended. Light from bare windows is not flattering to her. She may have been recently crying. She picks up a scrambled lump of newsprint from the floor. *Focused on Singles, Sock Delivers an Upset*. She doesn't get what it means, shakes her head. The room's dusty emptiness delivers an upset.

She looks around one last time and goes out to the hallway. Takes a grip on the doorknob, takes a breath, pulls it shut behind her. Locks each of the three locks they had installed to get cheaper insurance. Out of habit, pockets the keys.

"Hey." Young guy in a suit blends out from shadow. "Hey, Mrs. Rudge. The buyers will want those keys."

She hands them across without fuss. What can you do?

* * *

In this other building, the hallway light keeps going out. The old man in the green sweater—more holes than thread—tells her to keep jinking the switch, while he tries getting poorly-copied keys to make peace with an old lock. Each time the light coughs back on, it brings out the relief-scape of his head—thin, greased-down hair not concealing flaky welts and ridges of some specifically local, specifically this-town disease.

"It's a steal," he tells her, the umpteenth time.

"You walked right up on the sweet spot."

Margaret Rudge looks left and right down the hall-way—closed doors, dark turns veering off who knows where?

"Who else lives here?" she tries sounding informed.

Hunched, the old man glances back. "I'm the FBI now?"

Okay, the place is shabby. The couch sits low, like the legs wore down or got sawed through the middle. The single bed has a kind of mist floating above it. Someone has tried to decorate the bathroom tiles with stencils of Paris, which, worn through by wet and steam, appear as ghostly, grubby delusions. The bathroom window is internal; the other side looks like a stairwell someplace else in the building.

Gingerly, Margaret tweaks back the lounge curtain. There's not much to see. "It's how much a month?"

Affronted, the old man gestures at the fireplace. "Original fittings. Best you'll get this side of Jersey."

She scratches at the window glass. "Seems very dark outside."

"So? You can see the stars."

* * *

First night in a new place, too zonked to unpack. Cheap furniture almost sunk beneath cardboard boxes and trash bags of clothes. Curled on the couch, Margaret watches TV in a fluffy dressing gown and novelty bunny slippers, while digging deep in a family-size bucket of sweet popcorn. She is lit only by the TV—an old-school ray tube model. The motor of the DVD player on the stand is almost as loud as the soundtrack. Original fittings.

From the tinny speaker comes a big man's voice. 'Are you sure I can't offer you a coffee and a bear claw? They're very good. They're fresh.'

She smiles slightly. Snuffles. Shovels so much popcorn into her mouth she starts to choke, the kernels flying out like tasty shrapnel.

* * *

The sun shines on 5th Avenue and the old Public Library gleams like the seat of some benevolently conservative despot. Margaret, in a lightweight jacket and jeans, with a smidge of colour on her cheeks and her hair a little more brushed, catches sight of a sale on pant suits in a store window. Checking her reflection in the glass, she flicks up her brunette fringe, pulls down her eyebags, and grabs the back of her neck to pull her skin tight, mimicking Botox. The action draws a big, loopy grin from her large lips. Her tongue droops out like a dog's.

Behind her reflection, a shop assistant of the cute blonde type unhitches the concealed doorway into the window display. Now, this woman is young and very pretty, and working the store she dreamed of working since she was a kid pulling Saturday shifts in Kmart. Curious, she regards the older woman in the street, whose bulging eyes and lapping tongue seem a strange and not-quite comfortable approximation of Scooby Doo.

They make eye contact. With a sheepish grin—because she can actually grin and is good at it—Margaret hurries on to a sweet and swish little café on West 45th.

Alone in a booth, wanting to look occupied in the eyes of the bearded young techs and sharp funny girls all about, Margaret starts to untangle the *Times*, trying to filet it into some usable order. As she struggles against the baffling folds, its sections and inserts fall out. An especially solid wedge of paper unhooks and thunks to the table, detonating her latte in all directions. As liquid soaks the heritage newsprint, Margaret panics, grabs up a hunk of paper. It's the Personals.

The waitress glides over, slim and fresh-looking, like all the women there. She starts to mop the table, picks through the sodden paper. "Lonely hearts?"

"I was looking for the football. You rate the Giants this season?" Margaret attempts a flung ball-catching gesture, her smile like wax.

Scrunching up the paper, the waitress so-incidentally flashes a cute engagement ring. "You want the check?"

"I'm waiting for someone."

"We close two a.m. honey."

The open street door brings a swirl of interest from the booths—it's Cindy. She's Margaret's BFF, same age but every way younger, lighter, more a living presence in the city. Sort of woman that men love and women envy.

Cindy swings through the café like it's a catwalk, heads turn in sequence as she goes by. Mouthing a silent 'Hi' she slides sideways into the empty side of the booth. Manicured fingers detect the table is wet. "Been here long?" To avoid the damp plastic, she reaches over, squeezes Margaret's upper arm like trying a muscle. "Is that thick material?"

Sensing new opportunity, the waitress returns.

Cindy beams at her. "Naked latte. I won't be eating."

The waitress stares for a slight, slack-jawed second. "I'll tell the cook to get his coat." As she walks off, she slaps the side of her head.

Cindy watches primly, then turns to Margaret, mouthing, "Pregnant," before switching to full volume.

"We have so much to talk about. Your divorce. Oh, I was so sorry. When you seemed so used to each other. All for some girl who's young and interesting. He'll be sorry. Did I tell you about Gerry?"

Margaret stares glumly at Cindy's busy mouth.

There are now several empty cups on the table. Cindy has been talking about Gerry awhile.

"Then he had me swing off the side of his boat. Salt air is so invigorating. After that, we banged two days solid. The hotel called the Fire Department."

Margaret sits motionless, hands in her lap.

"Is that the time? Must run. You know how it is. Really, you should start dating again. Before you put on weight. There are some great apps now, you can have any man under your finger."

"I don't know." Really, Margaret doesn't know. "Maybe I'll wait a while."

Cindy gets stern.

"Yeah, and next thing you know, you'll be wearing slippers and eating take-out." That heavy whisper kicks in. "And you're not exactly a Millennial are you, dear? There are great creams for eyes these days. Though surgery's better. Little smooth and slice, who knows what you get."

"I could join a club or something."

"No need. Totally. No. Need," like sharing important secrets, Cindy hunkers in. "You know where young people pick up? At the store, on the subway, at coffee carts. Anywhere they're waiting in line, eyes meet. The whole city's a dating service. Everyone hooks up waiting for their latte."

Never happened to Margaret. "They do?"

"My friend Bree—you know Bree?—she was saying about this lovely old man who has a cart down in the East Village. East 7th, Avenue A—somewhere exotic. Cutest young guys queuing up for espresso, just waiting for a bit of this," Cindy fusses her hair, "bit of that," she does something with her eyelids. "You can take your pick."

"You can?"

"Of course. The old guy's so busy there, you're at least ten minutes in line. Been a dream to dialogue. Message me. Ciao." Cindy leaves, tinkling her fingers.

Watching the blond swan out, the waitress slings the check in Margaret's lap.

"She late for a client or something?"

Hazily, Margaret fumbles at the check. Double-takes at the bottom line. "Is there some mistake here?"

The waitress gives her a steady look.

"How far back you want to go?"

2.

$\int$ ince the day Frank got this pitch, everyone's told him the place is dead. If not dead, dying. If not dying, then nothing like it was in the sixties, the thirties, when Hamilton's old lady lived here, whatever whatever. People always say St. Marks, East 7th, Alphabet City, it's over. Same people who never imagined a world where choosing from a hundred flavors of coffee would be a human right. Yep, thinks Frank, packing his stand at the end of the day, all in all he done right, trading his soul into the coffee game.

The stand packs down to minimal space. He dismantles everything non-fixed. Unhooks the syrup bottles, stows cardboard cups in his small truck. Frank has the leathery look of outdoor life and a physique from doughnuts.

In the corner of his eyeline, an odd-looking woman bobs around, making puppyish faces. It's been a tough day, Frank's getting old and long ago lost any need for politeness. "Sling it lady, I got pasta fazool and a younger woman waiting."

Dodging around him, Margaret starts closing the lids of boxes he hasn't even finished with yet. She unhitches a bottle of almond syrup. "I was just wondering."

"Lady, if you got troubles there's numbers you call. I had enough bums dicking me out. I been rushed solid twelve hours."

"Yeah," Margaret perks up, "that's what I wanted to ask you about."

Stock still, Frank gives her a heavy look.

"I already said to you. No."

He keeps loading his truck while Margaret buzzes at him, a perky, pesky gnat.

"You built so much goodwill here. I could help out."

Abruptly, he turns at her.

"And what? What exactly do you know about this game?"

"I like coffee."

There's that grin.

"You like coffee?"

"I helped in a soup shelter last Christmas. Recent experience, huh?"

He slams the tailgate, letting its echo hang the length of East 7th. "This is not a hobby. Takes skill. Dedication. Money. You got money?"

Just a little, her warm face cracks.

"I got my settlement."

"Layoff?"

"Divorce. Though I got laid off too. He went to Canada."

"Your ex?"

"My boss. He's a fugitive from justice. My ex went to Phoenix. Found that out when I got served the restraining order." A new bargaining chip presents itself. "I work cheap."

"How about free. I pitch at five. You heard of five in the morning?"

"Oh sure, I do a lot of my crying then."

"Let's not bring it to work, huh?"

"Thank you so much. You won't regret it." As Margaret reaches to shake his hand, she drops the bottle of almond syrup. It shatters on the sidewalk, splashing their legs.

Frank regards the broken glass, the sugary gunge setting hard on his pants. "You change jobs often?"

"Oh look." Margaret points, delighted. "Licking your shoe. Is that a squirrel or a rat?"

Regular passersby in the next few days might notice how Margaret's induction into the coffee stand life is progressing. There she is, turning up late for work, getting shouted at by Frank while he waves his watch in his face. And later, she flips down a lever on the espresso machine and water cannons herself. The stand has a good trade in pastries. See Margaret, serving a doughnut with her thumb in the jam. And when she turns up late again, Frank presents her with an alarm clock. It's a fast-paced business and even these youngsters still sometimes pay cash. Which is why there's a lot of hand-waving and shouting about wrong change, while Margaret looks on, perplexed.

Long hours, physical business. Back at her grimy rental, she sits on the couch struggling to yank her shoes off. With an especially vigorous heave-ho, one shoe flies across the room, hitting one of the landlord's dismal pictures. It falls from the wall and shatters. Margaret stares at it, surprised, then gets the tang of her foot. She folds her knee under to sniff her toes. "Hey Mario! Extra Parmigiano!" Then she giggles, then she stops. She sits staring at nothing at all.

* * *

Next morning, bright and early, Frank is on his cellphone engaged in his real business.

"Four hundred on number three in the two-ten, a treble-double on four and seven in the two-forty-five. Yeah, with an accumulator. Tax? Stan, you're killing me."

Single-handedly running the stand, Margaret has a line of customers, who notice that her novelty baseball cap with a functioning propeller on top pushes her hair out awkwardly like a clown's.

Skipping over the kids tuning back in from last night's reefer, commuters on cellphones, and would-be music promoters, halfway down the line is David Scott. Mid-twenties, athletic, in must-have jacket and on-trend hair, he wears shades though it's cloudy and still he looks cool. Underneath that jacket he's a honed machine.

Margaret's had lectures from Frank about sales technique. Eye contact, cross-selling, creating that divine ease where customers just have to say 'The usual'. She's working on eye contact, separating her gaze from whatever her hands are doing. So, she glances up quick and thinks she sees a heavyset guy in a long coat and shades across the street. Maybe chewing a fat cigar. Margaret is entranced. "Buck Russell!"

By now, David is head of the line. Margaret catches her distorted reflection in his shades. "Coffee and a bear claw? They're very good. They're fresh."

That puzzles David. He's new to this street, this corner. "Flat white. What did you say?"

Oh that grin, it spreads inanely through Margaret's face. "You don't want one and I don't need one."

Which, unsurprisingly, David finds more disconcerting. He's late and concerned as to what kind of neighbourhood this is. "Yeah. Can I get a flat white?"

To Margaret, it's a puzzle why the penny still hasn't dropped, so she pitches the next line.

"You better know I'm bigger than you."

"Look, excuse me?"

Okay, so he's not going to get it. Perhaps it was her delivery.

"Career Opportunities," she says brightly. "The movie."

David feels this might be dangerous and drops his voice to a calm, assuring tone. "Is there someone else I could talk to?"

Behind him, a certain restlessness convulses the line, not entirely helped by watching the propeller spin on Margaret's hat, or by the fact that Margaret is grinning fit to bust. "What's your favourite Candy? John Candy!"

If there's anything that really vexes David, it's getting his cool ruffled in public.

"I don't eat candy, I'm on a special...who's John Candy?"

That's it. Margaret's beaming face crumples quick as a child who's burst its balloon. "Who's John Candy?"

"Friend of yours? What?"

Margaret, her voice steamrollered flat. "I saw a guy looked like Uncle Buck. Thought it was a sign."

Slowly, David nods, sets a note down on the counter. "Keep the change."

* * *

On the couch that night, in Bugs Bunny PJs, Margaret watches a movie with the lights off. That same big man's voice. 'If your kid spills his milk do you slap him in the head?'

She leans back into the sofa, deflated.

3.

Too early on another cloudy East Village morning, all the warmth of summer whipped away as winds from the big gray sea promised nothing but winter. Hugging the machines to chase chills from her bones, Margaret serves coffee, pushes pastry, tries to look bright and in control. Till she sees David walk by, far side of the street, carrying some other place's take-out cup.

The apron is gone from her waist. "Got to go pee." She grabs a convenience store bag from under the counter. Takes a bear claw from the rack.

Frank watches her skitter out between traffic.

"If you're pregnant you're fired."

Turns to his next customers, a pair of female cops. They glare at him.

"What?"

Busy morning on Avenue A, brisk crowds headed for the subway, going to work in the streets south of East Houston where art meets money and money rolls up in delight. Under trees just starting to shed their shadowing leaves, it gets difficult for Margaret to keep tabs on David.

Occasionally, she jumps up to see he's still walking ahead, not even registering the concerned looks she gets from passersby.

Close as she dares, Margaret tracks him, left into Stanton, right into Suffolk, to an old warehouse. He yanks open the black painted door and goes in. It shuts behind him with a tight thud. Trying to keep cool, to contain her excitement at being so successful a stalker, she sprints across to the warehouse, checking with bemusement the sign by the door: Contemporary Dance Theater. Her legs can't resist attempting a hoofer's grapevine, but her knees lock and she has to grab at the wall not to fall down. The door isn't locked, so it must be okay to go in, right?

In fact, these are the outer doors. Inside, there's another pair, glass, pinned back, with a closed-up hatchway to one side labelled 'Box Office.' In the circulation space beyond, a few tables and chairs are set around a bar counter, also closed. The walls have large glossy posters of men in tight pants and women in nothing stretching their bodies to vast, heroic poses. Lot of shots of black leotards and gray dresses doing backflips and summersaults—attitudes that look submissive and menacing all at the same time. Interspersed with the pictures are pleas for sponsorship, for funding to secure the future of, quote, 'this unique and precious resource'. Eyes widening, she realizes that she's stumbled into high-end showbiz.

Hauling open another black door, getting tangled—only briefly—in black curtains, she tumbles into the auditorium. House lights are up, reflecting dully off black painted walls, illuminating the simplicity of the central stage. Chairs and crates are stacked around the edge of the room. Peeking down one of the corridors, she glimpses a brightly-lit rehearsal space, a mirror showing reflections of young men and women doing stretches. They are lithe, muscular, filled with potential energy.

Retreating to the shadows, intrigued, conscious not to get found, she follows a dingy corridor to an open doorway labelled 'Male Change,' scrunching her face at this strange instruction. Down deep in the warehouse there's no natural light. Like any change room, it's a landscape of lockers and benches, notices about tidiness, about security, tacked to the walls, along with tightly printed want ads for dance instructors, movement specialists, assistant stage managers, and summer camp counsellors. Though alert for options, Margaret doesn't feel qualified even for the dispiritingly-described opportunity of free study in return for studio cleaning. She turns her attention to inside the change room.

David sits on a bench. He's unbuttoned his shirt. His torso is hard and smooth.

In the gloom by the doorway, Margaret is transfixed. How young he is. How flawless. She cups a hand from her mouth to her ear, whispering pep-talk advice.

"Don't get pushy on the first date."

Then she jumps into the room, waving the bear claw doughnut and growling. "Fresher than the average bear!"

With a primness that's frankly ludicrous for a man of his age and beauty, David grabs a towel from the bench.

As he yanks it towards him, his coffee cup goes bowling across the tiles.

Margaret watches the liquid spin out.

"Should have brought you a flat white. I never forget a beverage."

By now, David's on his feet, loud and indignant.

"What are you doing in here?"

It's surprising to Margaret she should have to explain. "I thought we got off on the wrong foot yesterday. I came to make up."

Aware of, and irritated by, his hyperventilation, he swallows down hard. "Are you okay?"

To Margaret, that sounds an opening.

"Fine. Couldn't be better. Just loving being single in the city. Don't you? If you are. Single, I mean. Are you gay?"

"What?"

"Not that it stops me. I got these."

She waves the plastic bag.

"Movies. John Candy's greatest. You can borrow 'em. Hell, keep 'em. I'll just rip 'em off the net."

She reaches for the deep voice. "'I'm Uncle Wart.'"

Makes quote marks with her fingers. "'Melanoma Head.' That always kills me."

In the years since leaving college, if David thought he'd ever get cornered in a change room again, he didn't figure it would be some crazed older woman, brandishing cultural references he doesn't get. He tries to gauge how fast he could be to the hallway. "I think I'll just get someone now, okay?"

Rummaging through her extensive stock of facial expressions, Margaret finds a look of engaged concern.

"As for *Planes, Trains and Automobiles*, he acted Martin off the screen in that. Off the screen. Don't you think?"

She gestures at him with the bear claw. How can he dodge around that?

"Believe me, I don't know what you're talking about. But now I have to rehearse."

"Dancing?" She grins. "I love to dance. I got disco feet."

She tizzes her fringe, does something weird with her eyelids. "Would you have coffee with me?"

"Good God no."

Music down the hallway and young, springing limbs.

Fighting over the hurt, Margaret tries to save something, some clue to how this happened. "Do I come across as a little anxious?"

Keeping safe distance, David moves by, the towel clutched tight to his torso.

"Honey, you come across like some lady with fifteen cats."

"Cats?"

"I got to go plié."

As he rushes by, she calls after him, "Break a leg! Or not!"

The change room lights throw her shape on the grungy tiles. "He called me honey. That's progress, right?"

Carefully tucking the bag of DVDs into David's locker, she attempts a dancer's twirl, slips on the spilled coffee, and sprawls, watching the bear claw slide away under a bench.

* * *

Some people get all their shopping delivered and that says everything there is to be said about them. Some people only go big brand places. They take a cab home, broadcasting love for their precious labels. Some drive a hundred miles for a discount and call anyone stupid who doesn't.

In matters of retail, Margaret Rudge doesn't have those choices. Her apartment building, in some side-lined part of the Bronx which no greening initiative reached, sits on a street truncated one end by a railroad yard that, in the dark, stretches and clanks and groans far into the distance. The street narrows to an unlit footbridge over the lay-up tracks, which she hasn't yet had cause or courage to cross. Leaving the bus and walking down from the other end of the street there's a Jamaican restaurant spilling music that itches her toes, a laundromat where a toothless old woman scrutinizes her clothes with distaste, and a convenience store. One of those neighbourhood stores, selling everything from vanilla to liquor, with plastic tables set outside where, by day, old men smoke and drink coffee they claim never tastes like it did in their fictional youth. It's by night, though, that the place comes alive, with sneaker tops, skate blades, and girls whose mauve blusher says they'd just spit on a mall rat. It's the Moonlight Supermart where Margaret shops.

She goes in, still feeling the bruises of the change room floor. She has another ache too, in her heart. It's often there.

The store is shabby, its stock chaotic, but there's out of date packets and tins on discount—not that Margaret likes to cook. Not, in fact, that her husband liked to eat what she cooked, which is why he chased extra business so she didn't have to. She doesn't buy much, some milk, some cheese, oranges because she's heard too many vitamin scares, a cereal pack for a chance to win a vacation at Universal Studios Florida. There's a Best of Daria DVD on the rack, but she doesn't feel strong enough yet. Margaret carries her groceries in her arms, as a brake on impulse buying.

At the cash desk, a chunky, jowly man argues with the clerk about really quite a minor mistake in his change. Margaret is often involved in this sort of argument and she feels the impulse to intercede, to bring them together through empathy, but really they're having too much fun ripping the piss from each other.

"You go to school? Learn to count, fool? Eleven dollars fifty-seven cents, what's hard about it?"

"I don't have a twenty in the tray. You say you give me twenty. I don't have a twenty. Didn't you try this last week?"

"What's that mean?"

"We had this same conversation last week."

"We did not."

"The camera shows..."

"Listen, boy."

The man sets a mighty, wobbling arm on the counter. "Don't tell me what the camera shows. Don't tell it."

Sweeping up his nine-dollar shopping, he swings his bulk around and collides into Margaret, standing just behind him. Her groceries spill on the floor.

"Watch where you stand you loony bitch. I got glandular issues."

She lets it go, along with his taste of sweat and defeat. Crouching to retrieve her things, she doesn't notice, not straight away, Bobby the night clerk arrive.

Bobby works night shift, one of those stringy, curly-haired pale boys that have no substance by daylight. He has a Vonnegut paperback in his coat pocket and clothes that all look the same. He graduated NYU, a philosophy major, thought he'd stay in town for summer. He's thirty-two now.

Smooth as autopilot, he hunkers down his skinny legs to help Margaret gather her shopping. Yes, they crouch close to each other. Yes, their eyes meet. No fireworks, though. Wrong time, wrong part of time. They gaze at each other like solitary, curious children.

"You have everything, Miss?"

Whatever hometown voice he once had has been drowned by New York rain. He points under the chiller.

"That baloney yours?"

Margaret squints to see.

"I think it was there when I got here."

He doesn't help her up. That would be intrusive.

* * *

A few nights later, Margaret is all dressed up, her one good pant suit carefully pried from its cleaning wrap. She's washed her hair in the grimy water that fitfully spurts from the bathroom faucet. Now she's attempting the unfamiliar task of makeup. She picks and paws at the wall mirror. "Damn glass, covered in lines."

She rehearses what she'll say. "So, we got off on the other wrong foot. Wrong foots run in my family. So, I came to cheer you along."

She considers. It's not enough. "You were great. In that dancing. Really great."

Her smile fades.

* * *

There's a ripped, hip young crowd blocking the street back to Rivington. Chattering brightly, such fine, big plans, such wonderful futures waiting. Everyone here is an artist, even those who don't work a lick. Each one their own creation, as heftily managed and curated as a big-ass MOMA show or a political stunt.

Honestly, Margaret doesn't look bad in the crowd. Her suit is dark, her hair has its own scruffy funk, she's not so overweight that people part round her. Thing is, though, she's alone. The art lovers laugh and wave 'Hi' to friends over the street. Halfheartedly, Margaret does the same. But to no one. As she gets near the door, she waves at some indeterminate shadow. "Tweet me," her voice hoarse.

Young men in black shirts and good skin funnel the crowd at the entrance. Breathing tight, clinging hard to her place in the mob, she pops through the door, riding the hustle toward the auditorium. The bar area has vanished completely beneath the crowd.

At the inner door, another young man checks tickets. Baffled but resolved, Margaret faces him.

"One please. You have a discount for essential workers?"

As so often, her words are met with a shift towards wary concern.

"Can I see your ticket?" He ponders. "Madam."

"I don't have a ticket. I need one. Please."

This young functionary of Terpsichore grows more bemused.

"The show sold out weeks back. You need a ticket."

By now, a bottleneck of bodies is jammed around them, so tight that Margaret can barely wing out her elbows from her hips.

"Sold out? How could it? It's the opening night. Sold out? That's just silly. I mean, no one buys a movie ticket till they see what the fat guy says on TV."

He gauges this, against the recognizable faces of his peers, waving tickets.

"You know," cold stealing across his voice, "you might feel more comfortable outside."

But here comes something not unlike salvation. It's Cindy, dressed in something daringly split three places. She has the body for it. Greasing along beside her is the most appalling old geezer, heavily minted, in wraparound shades, dressed thirty years too young. Cindy's face registers brief alarm, quickly sliding to society-neutral.

"Margaret! What a surprise! Is your television broken?"

Cindy goes in for an air-kiss. Margaret doesn't understand what she wants and just stands there. She grins glumly.

"I came for the dancing. But it sold out."

"Fabulous!" Cindy claps her hands girlishly, "Come with us! Gerry is a trustee here. He likes to encourage young people. You can be our guest, can't she Gerrikins?"

Gerrikins makes no discernible choice about it.

Cindy beams, stroking his face.

"So moist! Come along, Margaret. I'll tell you all about what Gerry keeps in his sub-basement."

"Lovely."

With a fixed smile, Margaret follows them through the velvet rope.

* * *

What does Margaret see, the next hour and a half? Of course, on the plain old superficial, everyone sees the same thing: a carefully-selected, exquisitely-performed program of modern dance. Students take notes and fans gasp in awe at the audacious, ambitious, ground-breaking work of a company at the top of its game, epitomized in its two leads—lithe, focused, precise David Scott and wild, limber, commanding Larissa Lamar. Reviews will

[29]

focus on her coolly-expressive technique, will compare her to other female leads who, just a few years before, were the next big rave. Intense and short, the life of the dancer. A brief and brutal fame.

There's all this lingo and explication to describe skillful moving to music. That isn't what Margaret sees. She sees a man in his brash, accomplished prime, unselfconsciously and unselfishly fixing his limbs to the space around him, letting himself be scrutinized for every misfire, every misstep, wanting nothing back but some folks in the dark to slap their palms together. The specifics of movement, the grace and control Margaret could never manage. She follows his every step and is frustrated when he's relegated upstage to serve in the chorus. She doesn't want to see these other dancers. Especially, she doesn't want to see Larissa Lamar. In the final clinch where they pas de deux, Margaret's nails dig into the seat of her chair. She's one of the first to her feet for the standing ovation, trying to catch David's eye, to look friendly and familiar. Guess, though, he's blind with the lights.

After the show, the same bright chattering as before spills into the night. Cindy glides along on Gerry's arm, uptalking like her neck depended on it, getting trapped in an upward spiral of near-inaudible pitch. Gerry doesn't respond or react in any way.

In a physically obvious, heavy afterthought, Cindy recalls Margaret, aimlessly drifting at her side.

"Sure we can't give you a ride, dear?"

"Thanks. But I get a bus just eight blocks from here."

As Gerry propels her toward his Hellcat, Cindy lets a quick and careless kiss blow over her shoulder.

"Must run. Gerry's churning with choreography. Been a dream. Ciao ciao."

"Chow." Margaret flaps a paw, the crowd breaking round her.

She hangs, letting the crowd fade into the night, letting their laughter dissipate on the damp air. Till the stragglers are gone, till the young men in black shirts close the doors, and the street subsides to dripping darkness.

Hands in her pockets like a sad kid, Margaret steps and stumbles down the alley beside the warehouse, to where her snooping has discovered the Stage Door. She finds an old-school metal trashcan, perches on its complaining lid, lazily beating a rhythm between her knees. "Shave and a haircut. Two bits. Shave and a haircut. Two bits," as rain starts seeping down.

By and by, the stage door opens, the dancers leave, talking over each other. Margaret jumps up, the trashcan clanks over. Her voice is hoarse with disuse. "You were…"

The dancers walk on in a bright group. David and Larissa at the centre. Margaret coughs.

"You were great."

Some stop and turn. The group grinds about to face her.

Nervous under their charmed gaze, her voice fails.

"You were great. That's all."

"C'mon," shouts someone, "before they stop serving."

4.

____

Nearly ceremonious, making a call on her cellphone, because the thing is so rarely used with so many apps she'll never need nor understand. Days of serving coffee in the gathering fall cold. Nights scrutinizing old movies and cartoons for what to do. So different from when she got married a dozen years before, when she was a regular klutz and Tommy had that Honda dealership and plans for an empire. For a time she was even his 'beautiful, clumsy wife' in party introductions, his essential component that made his honest dealer act complete.

Ironically, it was Tommy who encouraged her to get a job with Jack Nertland's Frisky Shower Dog Spa and Boutique. Though Jack also branched into horses, but that didn't fit the name right. Not that she was actually allowed near the four-legged money-makers. A tad surprising she got the job doing Jack's accounts, it made a little more sense now. Now the police of two countries knew that Jack was also doing his accounts, a somewhat different way. As she told that rather bewildered detective, it hadn't crossed her mind the kennel maids were hookers. Lots of jobs have a dress code.

Time zones were just invented to bemuse her. Two a.m. in the Bronx, so it was, who knew, ten, eleven in Phoenix? Somewhere still looking forward to Jimmy Kimmel. The restraining order, though a surprise, and written in some odd language she barely understood, gave her a needless heads up on her ex's location. It wasn't sensible to call him, of course. It was two in the morning and raining, and Margaret had a big hole where her heart used to be.

Strange, soon as the call is picked up, she just knows it's someplace warmer, just something about the rustles and clicks in the background, cars honking loud, said open windows, and maybe that was the clink of ice in a glass. She scrambles after her lively voice, "Hey Tommy! How's motel life?"

"You evil, braindead witch. Don't you go to jail if you break your order?"

So this wasn't Tommy, then, but Juliette, the cognitive psychology intern who'd come to test-drive a hybrid and never brought it back.

"I can't believe how stupid you are calling this number."

Okay, so this was a setback. "Can I speak with Tommy? Please."

"Of course you can't you fucking moron. He needs complete rest. He actually twitches when he hears your name. A visitor came in today called Margaret and when he heard that, he needed lithium."

"Is he okay now?"

"None of your fucking business. They should give you the electric wire treatment, run it through your vacant head. Don't call this number again."

"Could you give him a message?"

"Fuck you."

"Hello? Hello?"

Okay, not good then. So, when Margaret curls up on the floor, maybe she's just tired. So, when there's a little wet patch of tears, maybe she has dirt in her eye. She stays there all night, sponging up damp, dreaming of dancing.

* * *

Next morning, while Margaret stands in the blistering cold, cheery as she can be dishing out danishes, Letasha Wilkins, manager of the Contemporary Dance Theater has an unwelcome visit from Clyde Demaria, a lawyer representing Sheridan Ringley. That's Sheridan Ringley, only direct surviving descendant of the nineteenth century Broadway impresario whose charitable endowment picks up a big wedge of the dance theater's costs. Ms. Ringley has lately turned twenty-five, she's taken control of her trust fund, and is deeply unimpressed with the family finances.

"I don't say it means anything bad." Clyde struggles with layman-speak. "Ms. Ringley has to be fully appraised of the endowment's situation. It's a question of sustainability."

Letasha Wilkins came at this art business the hard way. An Edgewater fly-girl in her youth, running with Hindu bad boys, she spent a couple years away for moving some packets she should really have let stay put. It was the prison-visiting dance teacher gave her the bug, as well as practice in saying 'No' politely to lesbians. Her degree in arts administration much fresher on the wall than many her age, Letasha of course understands commercial pressures as well as she understands the maze of funding and corporate incentives for healthy and active lifestyles. Unhelpfully, though, she doesn't like lawyers, nor trillionairesses younger than her.

"What we have is a sustainable resource, Mr. Demaria."

"Clyde, surely."

"Currently, we are hosting one of the country's hottest companies. You've seen PBS, the review in the *Times*."

"Does that come before the Sports section? Look, Letasha. Ms. Wilkins. The endowment was created off the back of substantial commercial activity. Ms. Ringley's forebear was one of the biggest on Broadway."

"I'm sure."

"He was deeply concerned for sustainable art."

"If Wikipedia is to be believed, he was also deeply concerned for burlesque and minstrel shows."

"Yes, if it's to be believed."

"Darktown Delites was one of his."

"With an authentic cast, I believe. Which brings me to the nub of Ms. Ringley's concerns."

Letasha's worked hard for this. She read all the motivational books. She knows to keep her emotions on slow burn.

"Go on, Mr. Demaria, I'm interested to know."

"During the current residency, what's the," darn layman-speak again. Clyde baulks at these street words. "What's the demographic of your crowd?"

"Well, we don't do a survey with the tickets."

"Do you not?"

"But I would say, it's people who love modern dance. A young crowd." She's been at the bar with them. "Definitely Millennial."

"Of wide ethnicity?"

"Like a fucking tutti-frutti." Edgewater, it breaks through some times. Her analyst says don't sweat it. "We have people of every conceivable colour and every permissible gender. We have drag acts and fag hags more whippy than Gloria Vanderbilt. We had a matinee for the Hampton seniors. They loved it."

Letasha gets that she's cooking a little too hot, so she picks up her phone and thumbs round the screen to grab some insouciance back. Can't resist just dropping one more, though.

"How long has Ms. Ringley lived out in Columbus?"

This gets Clyde on the lawyer high horse.

"My client's domicile is neither here nor there. Her concerns, however, are pertinent. It's about sustainability. About widening access."

Damn, but these are her own kind of words, flung back at her like ninja stars. All her training goes into the care of picking words. "Are you saying Ms. Ringley wants us to widen access?"

"Go a little more popular, yes."

"Dumb down?"

Tabloid talk, damn she shouldn't have.

"Not at all. Just a program better pitched at the average fan."

Clyde Demaria picks up his briefcase.

"She told me she'll drop by Saturday night. To get a feel for how the place is going."

Letasha needs to know what he means by that, what exactly he thinks he's saying. But Clyde, he's delivered his client's message and, with clammy relief, takes a cab to the lower 20s, where the mistress he's been seeing the last ten years stirs daiquiris and busts his balls.

* * *

The same moment Clyde's walking out, the dance company is taking a break from rehearsal, a strict fifteen to fuel on water, make calls and maybe, just maybe, spend a minute or two longer than most in the toilet. David has no plans beyond checking the grip of the support bandages on his legs. The season's going well, full houses, good reviews—that PBS special sealed the second week. Not a seat to be had for face value.

Dancers have a pain threshold beyond the average mortal. Constant repetition of exaggerated movements means a level of strain considered illegal in Federal interrogations. At least here they're doing a tight, intense repertoire, not some sprawling classic. The pay barely covers a wheatgrass smoothie in this town. Oh, but it's better, so much better, than what he came from. Than the streets he did everything to run from, before running became a dance.

This theater though—none of the spaces, the hallways, have natural light. The whole backstage is neon and shadows. Times when he's tired, when fatigue's kicking up, feels like he's underground, an endless warren without sunlight, without the stiff wire brush of city air to bring him around.

David squints up, trying to steady his eyes on the most liquid, unmissable sight. Larissa Lamar, in the open doorway. She's been on fire these nights, her picture next to the *Times* review quite rightly. Principal female, more a star than anyone on that stage. Supple, expressive—an exquisite dancer. Right at the age where she has to make big—has to, before the swift fall to earth like the spent fuel tank of a one-time rocket. They're sharing some crampy Airbnb this fortnight—just splitting the rent. There's too much serious work for wasting time. Larissa is beautiful and a little cruel. What an ace.

"I don't think Susan is progressing," she says, meaning one of the other dancers. "Her arch has no more clarity than it did the first night."

David isn't sure what to do with this information. He nods because Larissa requires agreement.

"Adam needs to work more on his effort economy. He's flagging by halfway through the third piece."

"He's had a rough time. His mom, you know, with the milk boy and the Quaaludes." David likes Adam.

Even when Larissa frowns, there's a willed, meaningful flow to the movement of muscles.

"I don't *pas de chat* with his mom."

Larissa's on the bench beside him. She wasn't, then one lightning move and she was. "I don't want to waste my time."

He's heard this before and strongly suspects she said the same to her teachers in grade school. Again, David nods, not thinking—not consciously—of the extent to which he's a collaborator in her opinions.

"I was going to tell you this tonight." Her voice travels down his spine. "I meant to save it, but that arch."

"What's on your mind?" It comes out surprisingly curt.

"This company is respected," she drops to a whisper, "we all know that. The reviews, the exposure, all great."

"There's a but?"

"Respect doesn't pay rent. I've worked hard, we both have." Just a brief touch on his arm, but the feeling stays. "I had a call, after the *Times* piece. Pfeiffer, in Berlin."

"Pfeiffer?"

"Berlin. All that borrowed cash, looking for modern dance."

"Pfeiffer himself?" He knows he sound dumb. The bell is already ringing.

"Yes," Larissa looks surprised. "Pfeiffer knows how to use a phone. He offered top billing, pay, an apartment. The most job security this side of hoofing in musicals."

Dirtily, David doesn't mind a musical.

"You going? To Berlin?" His voice sounds odd, like a boy getting dumped by his crush. ·

"Listen."

The bell is ringing.

"We'll talk tonight, but listen. I go over there, do a season or two, get the dressing room door. Tell Pfeiffer he needs a new male lead. I can do that."

"A season or two?"

"Get established, then tell him he needs a new male lead and I know just the guy. Your kudos will be sky high by then. Don't tell anyone, though."

"Like I would."

"I mean it." That sharpness, bracing her soft tones. "These guys are good, but they'll never be good as us. Let's use this time to make plans."

David watches her slide from the room, so nearly not touching the ground. Slings his muscle rub back in his locker. It lands with an unexpected hard crackle. That damn bag, still there. He wrestles it out from among the leggings and dance belts. A convenience store bag, wrapped around a wad of old-school DVDs. Movie titles he doesn't recognize: *Armed and Dangerous*; *Delirious*; *Planes, Trains and Automobiles*; *Uncle Buck*. Each garish cover bears a strip of Dymo tape—the raised, wobbly letters say 'Stolen from Margaret Rudge' with a slew of stars, exclamation points, and percent signs. The bag has a store name, Moonlight Supermart, splashed around with moons and Saturns. An address in the outer space Bronx.

5.

Though he never would have believed it, Frank has to admit that Margaret is growing a feel for the business. Now she burns people and bilks their change less often, and even impatient customers respond merely grudgingly to her ditzy moves. And the novelty baseball hats are a solid draw—Frank's favourite is the one with the hammer that looks so tantalizingly like it's striking her skull.

Anyhow, Frank has had some nice days at the horses, so he's feeling expansive.

"I don't mind at all," he tells Margaret, "you getting a job on the side. Still want you here five a.m. though."

"Oh yeah," she nods, bells on her hat jingling, "you know I'm super reliable. Would you write me a reference?"

"Get the job first," he counsels, "it might be with someone I like."

Truthfully, it's someone Frank doesn't know. He doesn't go to the dance. With a young wife and pasta fazool he stays home nights.

It's taken a lot, really sliced her, to get Margaret back on this street. It was the poster for the dance show, with a flash pasted across saying 'Closing soon' that gave her the kick for one last throw. Closing soon—how bad can it be? She'll make a fool of herself again and the dance will be done. Because Margaret understands that. She knows people think she's dumb. Ever since school, since before school, she's been falling over, colliding with walls, failing to get how being just what she is seems so hard for people. Sadly for her, she's a lost cause, a fatal case— an optimist in love with the movies.

This time when she pulls back the black-painted door, she hollers out, "Hello there? Anyone home?"

Music from the rehearsal space, quick then interrupted

as the director stops to correct this, to substitute that, doing stuff they all know matters.

She tries a deeper voice. "'Who wants an Orange Whip? Orange Whip? Orange Whip? Three Orange Whips.'"

That resonant word, whip, reaches Letasha in her office.

"'You don't understand! I didn't have any food! I had to drink the beer! I had to drink it in order to survive!'"

Margaret spins, off-balance, at the sound of an opening door. A smooth woman in a black day dress stares at her.

"Just reprising a scene from *Masters of Menace*. You know it? Huh?"

"Can I ask how you got in?"

This hectic female may be harmless, or packing mace.

"Same way as before. Margaret Rudge."

The offered hand feels vaguely like pastry.

"I'm looking for your Human Resource department. It's about a hiring decision."

"I'm Letasha Wilkins. I manage this theater."

"Ah." Margaret hadn't anticipated the boss, but that's cool too. "You have a great place here, you know? One of my closest friends, Cindy Styvechale, she's very wrapped with one of your trustees. I was here with them just the other night. For the dancing. You know what I noticed?"

"Why are you wearing a cap with bells on?"

"Oh that. From my other professional role. I'm in bulk catering."

"Bulk catering?"

"To bulk people. I was here the other night, with one

of your trustees and, you know, I couldn't help notice how awkward it was to find space at the bar."

Letasha follows the woman's clumpy gesture to the cracked wooden tables and chairs set up by the counter.

Margaret meantime is channeling her ex, when he was cool and had plans. "If I show you the best investment you ever seen, could you commit to it right now?" Tommy told her that was called the "demonstration close" among the guys he hung with at O'Grady's.

"What are you talking about?" Where was the janitor? Why didn't those pretty boys in their black shirts work daytimes?

"You're going to be so happy with what I'm going to tell you." The "power of suggestion close." Margaret, who truthfully hasn't thought this through, walks across to the little bar cubby and starts pulling the chairs around. They screech on the cement. "Just imagine we open this out a bit. Maybe move back that wall."

"It's structural."

"That wall, then. Any wall. Say we move it all a bit back, get some bench seating in here. You know kids love bench seating." Margaret nods furiously. "Just a few tweaks and twists and what you got here? A café-bar venue to make this place worth visiting."

"The *New York Times* said it's worth visiting."

"Exactly." Margaret beams. "Can you afford not to build on that? Why don't you give it a try?" The "puppy dog close", a sure-fire killer. "Just give it a try for the weekend. I have very strong credentials in this."

"Which are?"

"You know that coffee stand just up the way?"

Messages, calls, missed opportunities stacking on every device. "Lady, are you some fruit loop? You think I'll let you walk in and rejig my theater? For the weekend?" Blind shit, the weekend. Closing night. Sheridan Ringley, looking for demographics. "You think doing some work here will increase casual footfall?"

"Could be casual," Margaret nods. "Or wholly dressed up."

Again, that sprightly commotion. The dancers on break, heading out for protein water. David and Larissa, in deep conversation, sweep by.

"Oh hello there," Margaret bellows. "You going for pastry?"

David double-takes. "Why are you here?"

"I'm on the team." Margaret bounces on the spot, jingling.

Larissa, who hates being interrupted, shoots a look, sees nothing to care for. "Who's the schlub in the clown hat?" She chivvies David along.

"You know the cast?" Letasha feels somewhat unnerved. Running reckless through Jersey taught her so much— just not about moments like this.

"Oh yeah." Margaret's grin appears to extend beyond her face. "We dialogue all the time."

* * *

Even with her new job and favourite cartoons, Margaret feels restless. A *Flintstones* box set doesn't take so long and the time seems stubbornly fixed at ten-thirty. In the damp air of her tiny apartment she feels night slipping in, diverse and inviting. The dance show is only just finishing up, they'll be taking their bows, getting changed, heading off to whatever dancers do. She doesn't have any grasp on their physical regime and imagines they must suck a whole lot of glamour, between right now and morning. She suspects there's a valve that must be released—in some ways she's right. Fastidiousness is the deadliest genteel pressure.

Really is dark outside. Not only the windows are grimy, the whole neighbourhood seems to hoard darkness, giving room to the day only piecemeal, reluctant to countenance too much exposure. Can hardly see the street but, if she squints, there's a slip of light that's the convenience store. Her cheesy shoes back on her feet, she goes out.

Maybe it's just fall coming on, but always round here there's a damp to the air, a taste of rain impending. Margaret goes, hands in her pockets, head down against the nips and tugs of the wind. There's a line in the store so she walks right by, down to the end of the street.

Under towering arc lights, the train yard drifts in hazy, metallic mist. The tracks fan out like some fossil fern, spiralling to the upper deck, strings of silver cars looking boxy and odd, like they wandered beyond the tunnel mouth and don't have a clue where next. A few get slung around by motormen too small to see from here, the clanks of shunting metal ratcheting against the cold night.

Strung along the bridge, local kids stare down at the tracks. Speculating ways to hop the train, to ride without paying far as Broadway, far as Brooklyn, far as the city goes. But really they know the lines go there and back, there and back, and for all their formidable distance, not one of these trains ever really leaves, never hits the open rails.

Margaret pulls her coat around, clings a hand on the safety wire cage encasing the bridge. So no one jumps. So no one's sadness stops traffic. One of the kids creeps up on her, hesitating, unsure about her drawn, pulpy face. Almost kindly, he says, "Want to buy some weed?"

Distracted by the lights and damp, Margaret replies, "Doesn't that make you awfully hungry?"

The kid strums the wire. "Yeah. Yeah, I guess it does."

The Moonlight Supermart is quieter when she walks back, the old men's coffee dregs on the outside tables set as firm as their skin is flaky.

Bobby watches her on CCTV, she drops a cereal box, knocks over some cans, tries to stop one with her foot and sends it spinning against the ice chest. Her broad face is structurally bewildered, as though none of these things are connected with her at all. Tottering round the aisles, she dumps an armful of groceries on the counter.

"Something for the sweet tooth?" He indicates the cheery packets, so healthy when consumed as part of a balanced diet.

"Tough day," she confides.

Now Bobby, he's seen this woman, in her shapeless coat, her intractable hair always ridged or flattened some way. He's seen her delight at a new collectable card, her astonishment when towers of produce fall down as she brushes past. She has nice skin and looks to be a warm, redolent age.

"Why I work nights," he says. "Avoids tough days."

She's noticed this young man with his funny, curly hair. Looks like he doesn't sleep and doesn't mind that. One of those people who has the sense of being an ally, accepting all sides, chronically non-committal.

"Different, living round here too," she hazards. Not often does she get personal. "I had a house before. With my husband. He ran off with a shrink."

"What, like, a bald guy in loafers?"

"Cognitive psychology graduate. I'm told she can go all night."

"I go all night. Oh, right."

Bobby flusters with his hands. Been a long time since that history major out in Flushing, who dug *Star Trek* as much as he does.

"And I lost my job in accounts. Honestly, I didn't spot he was running a racket."

"Guess things are a bit tight right now."

"Yeah."

He hesitates, nearly chokes, then pushes himself on.

"The chocolate. It's on the house. Regular customer discount."

She stares at the chocolate; she stares at the man. "Is that some kind of new scheme?"

"For local residents. You are local?"

"Just in the building up there. With the sign about not using the basement steps."

"You're not in the basement?"

"Oh no, I'm top floor. Very handy for the water tank."

She embraces her shopping bag. "Drop by sometime. I don't see the neighbours, just hear them."

When she's gone up the road, when the sound of her knocking into the outside tables subsides, Bobby checks the price of the chocolate, empties his pockets, and counts the exact cost of it into the drawer.

* * *

Steam from Larissa's bath musses up the lounge windows. Not often Larissa takes a long soak, but she's earned it if anyone has. A faint scent of tropical blooms rides in on the steam, uplifting the shabby, not-quite-anyone's room.

While water splotches and pops round the tub, David has fired up the ancient DVD player, carefully clearing the dust of disuse from its slots. He's watching *Planes, Trains and Automobiles*. Steve Martin's saying, 'You choose things that are funny, or mildly amusing, or interesting'. Getting psyched, Martin yells, 'It's like going on a date with a Chatty Cathy doll'. David's no age to know Chatty Cathy, but he gets it, he gets the string-pulling shtick, it makes him smile. Then Candy, Candy says, 'I talk too much, I also listen too much. I could be a cold-hearted cynic like you. But I don't like to hurt people's feelings'. What you see is what you get.

"David," Larissa calls from the bathroom. "Be a sweetie, massage my back."

He gathers the DVDs, puts them back in the bag.

"David, I got knotty shoulders."

His phone rings. It's Adam, whose quiet voice has acquired a dusting of cement. "I was having a drink with Susan. You know anything about Larissa saying she wants to move on?"

So not the time for that conversation. "Adam, hey. It's late, you know. Let's talk tomorrow, okay? Let's talk then."

"Susan was saying she sounded pretty decided."

"Adam, I got to sleep just now. Hey," as afterthought, "you hear of a guy named John Candy?"

Huffy, because he wanted the conversation now, Adam asks, "David, where am I from?"

David's hunting for his jacket. "What? I don't know. What'd you say, man?"

"Where am I from?"

Why's he asking? "Toronto? You're from Toronto."

"It's like asking if I heard of moose. Candy's a god. What about this thing with Larissa?"

"Tomorrow, man. Got to go."

As he appears at the bathroom door, Larissa—up to her neck in suds—is a tad surprised he's clambering into his jacket. "Are you cold?"

"Just got to step out." Only now, it hits him how rarely he does anything that might surprise Larissa. They're not married, not even together, but it horribly feels like he's having to draw a deep breath and ask permission.

"Got to see someone."

"Why?" There's a definite barb to her voice now.

"Got an errand. Be a couple of hours."

He leaves one of the greatest female dancers of the age staring speechless as he slams the apartment door.

* * *

Turns out the subway doesn't exactly go where he's headed. Seems the yard at the end of the line makes it a forty-minute walk around, so he takes the bus the last four miles, each stop getting deeper into what feels to be lost country. The place had a lot of money spent, it's come right up in the world. The environment's getting airtime, there are waterfront parks. But one or two little nagging neigh-bourhoods remain, places that never got the memo on rebranding. So the graffiti walls aren't colourful tourist teasers, but actual gang tags. The litter that wedges between silent buildings and blows across empty lots isn't some statement in an art house installation, but a piece of real estate too cheap and useless to save. He walks under a rail bridge that once led to the yards, but is now a dead limb of a long-demolished service. Water drips down from the rusted girders. Doesn't feel like rainwater.

Walking straight and serious between two churned out apartment blocks that just break apart, wondering if he took a wrong turn from the bus, he gets that familiar sting in his spine. He's being followed. Experience says keep walking, keep the shoulders strong, keep walking. Any looking around, any breaking step and you're food.

The guys jog up beside him and it seems bizarre, but he gets a kick from seeing they're wearing tracksuits. Retro Filas from back whenever guys did that. They're some lean and waterproof zip-up army.

On minimal inspection, they determine he isn't local.

"Yo," says one, "not so fast. You looking for someplace?"

"Hey," David says pleasantly, "how you doing?"

"Well," says another, steering his elbow. "We could be doing better. Always better. We have expenses."

"Hungry mouths," says the third, moving up ahead. "And you just entered our tax zone."

"Tax zone?" Still keeping it light. "Come on, guys. I pay enough tax." Though they probably make more than he does.

The guy in front, the lead guy, he sees that time is getting wasted. He fills up space, his demands precise.

"Give us your cash, bitch."

There's a memory there, something that sits way back in the days before David could dance. When all he knew was he wanted to. When the only nourishment he could find was ambition.

"No," he hears his voice, distinct. "We're not going to do that."

The three guys in tracksuits hustle him round. Their playbook is hard-end persuasive.

"I recommend," the lead guy, in David's face, "you do as we say. You give us your cash, you faggot."

There it is, right on time. Blocking out fear and consequence, thinking nothing at all, David lets all his dancer's power flow in behind his right fist. He punches the leader into the street, jabs at the others, and runs between shattered buildings, through a forest of twisted cables, back to the street.

Now he can't hear their feet behind him, now he lets himself feel his right hand burn, fire ripping the ligaments, tearing pain through the carpals. Out of practice, sloppy technique, but he hit the guy real hard.

As danger recedes, pain enlarges. David stumbles along a dark street, lit by the Valhalla of a convenience store. He crashes through the doorway, appealing his hand to the skinny, surprised-looking dude at the counter.

"Broke my fucking wrist."

Bobby finishes serving budget hard liquor to two old gentlemen, who squawk and holler round David as they roll out. "Been fighting, young fella? That's not a break. I can show you fighting." They stagger off, trading punches that could only connect if someone held both of them still.

David slumps against the counter, laying his hand as flat as he dares for inspection.

"Might just be a fracture," says Bobby, practiced in nightlife injuries. "Does it hurt all through?"

"Yes. It does."

"Then probably it's not broke. You have insurance?"

"For fighting?" David grimaces. "No."

"You want an ambulance?"

"Too expensive. Can you call a cab?"

"I can." Bobby scratches his chin. "Be a while round here, though."

He pours David a shot, estimating how much to feed the cash drawer. "What you doing here, man? You visiting?"

In horror, David watches the lack of flex in his hand. Takes a slug of whisky and splutters it out.

"Looking for someone. Margaret Rudge."

Penny drops.

"This is the Moonlight Supermart? She gave me a bag from here."

"They're collectible?" Bobby's taken aback.

"She gave me some things in the bag. You calling that cab?"

"Margaret Rudge." Bobby understands. It hurts, he feels it. "So high? Solid shape? Wavy hair? Big smile?"

"Yeah, she lent me DVDs. I'm kind of in pain here."

"Be right back. Anyone comes in, tell 'em wait a bit, won't you?" A useful afterthought. "Who do I say you are?"

"David."

Bobby hurries up the street, hurting, feeling it. This man with his busted hand, leather jacket, sweet eyes, his neat physique—this man's a different league, a different planet. All the things similar about them, the things that make them men, mean nothing next to what makes them different. This guy doesn't work convenience. Would have been so easy for Bobby to say, 'I don't know a Margaret Rudge. Good God man, where do you think you are? There'll be no one of that name here'. So easy to say it, call the guy a cab, pack him and his hand on their way. But then, what would Margaret say, next time she came to the store? Where are all the history majors that dig Star Trek?

* * *

She's finished a bottle of wine and she's not sleepy. Restless, not even a late night rerun of *M*A*S*H* can hold her attention. She glares at the screen, "B. J. Hunnicutt bullshit. He was no Trapper," before scratching again at the window, trying to see out. There's a light in the apartment across the way. A figure slumps in a chair, looks like a Stormtrooper, an actual Stormtrooper from Star Wars. White, black at the joints and with a fat helmet. "Oh my." The figure sits motionless. "Maybe he's drunk." Margaret jumps. A knock at the door.

This is unprecedented. Nobody knocks at her door. Not the unseen neighbours with their strange domestic chorus. Not the landlord—she posts a check for the rent. The knocking comes again, hard and invasive. A voice shouts in a quiet but hectic way. Could be anyone. Must be trouble.

Swiftly, Margaret searches the kitchen drawers, finds a nutcracker, the most nearly lethal object she has. Getting found alone, that's terrible—who knows how many maniacs might stalk the halls of apartment buildings at two in the morning? So, the answer is not to be alone.

"Ten dollars? For a beautiful rifle like this?" Her *Doberman* voice needs some work, so she switches up to *Angels with Filthy Souls*. "I'm going to give you to the count of ten to get your ugly, yellow, no-good keister off my property before I pop your guts full of lead." *Who Framed Roger Rabbit* is a solid touchstone. She digs in, "Remember me, Eddie? When I killed your brother I talked. Just. Like. This." The high alto fails her though and she starts to choke, refluxed wine burning her throat.

The knocking and shouting get more urgent. She kicks over a chair to make noise, grabbing the door handle, "Give me those ruby slippers!" whipping back the door and there's Bobby.

"Hi," her voice fails to transition properly and she screeches, "What a lovely surprise."

"You're Margaret Rudge, right?"

"If I bounced a check on you, it'll all be sorted next week."

Even now, Bobby thinks he doesn't have to do this. He can make like he was just passing by. He loves *Who Framed Roger Rabbit*.

"Would you like a drink? I may have some, something left." Aimlessly, Margaret roots around.

"There's a guy at the store needs your help." Damn, but he can see his breath, see the shape of it changing his life. "Guy called David. He asked for you."

"David." Margaret stares, all attention. "At the store? Right now?"

"Asking for you. He's hurt his hand."

"Oh poor love."

Wholly unselfconscious, Margaret folds her hands on her chest. "Poor love, what happened?"

"He thinks it's broken."

"Okay, okay."

Bobby watches Margaret dive back at the kitchen drawer, tipping out forks and spoons, a melon baller, candles and matches, sandpaper, fuse wire, till she finds a roll of electrical tape. Then into the icebox, digging out a couple of popsicle sticks.

"Suck the ice off that, come on."

Bobby closes her apartment door—she's already three stories down. He catches up with her down the street, both of them sucking fruit ice like crazy off the sticks.

"You really rate this guy, huh?" He wishes he had a more meaningful way to say it.

"My heart says." She gobbles the ice down, stripping the stick. "But he's so different to me. He's cool and successful." She doesn't mention younger, doesn't want it to sound like it matters.

"Why not follow your heart?" What Bobby sees, her worried profile, her concern to reach this man no matter what. "After all, you're single. Childless. Middle-aged. Broke. Poorly housed. Insecurely employed. Who could be more equipped to follow their heart?"

"Gee." Her grin illuminates the grimy street. "You really think so?"

David has downed four shots of whisky, and sold forty cigarettes, two cans of soup, and a hammock.

"Hello you two. Margaret?"

"Give me that." She whips the ice stick from Bobby's fingers. "What have you been doing?" Syrup could be squeezed from her voice.

"Got in a fight." Unable to move his damaged hand, David makes a biffing motion with the other. "Three guys. Should have seen them. Pussies."

"You shouldn't be fighting. It's not very artistic. Now, we'll soon get you fixed." She starts to work on his hand, fashioning a splint from the two juice sticks, binding them to his fingers with electrical tape. "You know, you got such soft hands."

"Should you do that? I mean, might you cause damage?" Bobby goes all-out not to sound sour.

"Oh I used to do this all the time with my husband. He was always getting engine hoods slammed on his fingers. Guess what?" she whispers to David. "I'm working at the theater!"

"You're what? Ow."

"Stay still. This very nice woman, the manager, she says I can refresh the bar this weekend. We'll have potted plants and prints, don't you think? Maybe sell some CDs."

"Could you put my hand down if you're going to gesture."

"And hats. People love novelty hats."

David's reeling eyes lock on the bundle of electrical tape at the end of his arm. "My hand in there?"

"And the best part, I'm going to call it—Hit the Barre."

"You know, there's a place in Jersey called that."

"They won't mind. Publicity, right?"

Meanwhile Bobby is serving some drunk, who's come in for drink but wants to drink something different to what he's drunk on. Though he can't remember what he's drunk on. These are Bobby's people—forgetful drunks, fretful moms with babies who just won't stop, street girls tricked-out and closed for the night, goldbricking cops wanting chocolate and coffee. The cops always talk sports. When he's thirty-five, forty, he'll still be here and the crowd will still be the same. Anyone different, any like Margaret, already have someone. "You still want a cab?"

Margaret is scandalized. "This man's an artist. He needs an ambulance."

* * *

Takes the paramedics a while to find them—the street doesn't show up on Google or something. In the manner of paramedics, they say, "We'll take it from here."

"Oh, I have to come with him." Margaret bounces onto the tailboard. "He's a very valuable property."

In their dark uniforms, against the night, the guys are just bald heads and busy hands. "Not sure where you're going with that," hazards one. "Is he in some kind of trouble?"

"This guy is a major balletic."

She waves at David on the gurney.

"I'm his agent. Margaret Rudge. Of Rudge & Light-feather."

"Please," hollers David. "I'm in pain."

"Well, come along then," Margaret chivvies these skeptical men. "We want to get there before the drunks."

They don't even try to unwind the black tape bandage.

First tug, David yells that the adhesive is pulling his skin. Margaret sits by his head, occasionally, beamingly, patting his good arm.

"Very brave. Aren't you? Brave."

When the paramedic gets distracted by his phone, she leans closer to David's face. "So, first date, huh?"

He's in no position to argue.

"Did you really? Punch that guy?"

Strange, how glowingly warm her face is, how her eyes gleam, no more serious than a child's.

"I gave him an upsetter."

"Tough guy." She crinkles her nose, squeezes his bicep.

"I grew up in a small town."

Really? He's telling her this? While she prods his bicep?

"I was the arty kid in a town of inbreds. Got called a fag and pushed around. That doesn't happen to me anymore."

For a moment, as the ambulance jogs and weaves through the morning streets, Margaret lets herself feel that hand on her arm, lets its warmth give her blood new rhythm.

"When I married, my husband loved me a lot. Really, really a lot. Called me his beautiful, clumsy wife. Then he stopped doing that. Ran off with some girl with a future."

"You have a future." Can't hurt to say it.

Margaret's smile dissolves in a watery melt.

"I think you mean you. You have the future."

"Last stop, folks," the driver calls. "Lincoln Hospital."

"Is this on your insurance?" David whispers.

"We'll think of something."

* * *

Life is about experience, tasting all the new fruit. Meeting new people and learning sufficient tolerance not to bust their skulls. Where's better for that than a city hospital emergency department at two in the morning? The doctors take pictures and know without troubling their swanky equipment that David's not really so injured. Not so much as some of the accident prone around him. They check him for trauma, shine lights in his eyes, make notes in a manila file. Doesn't take long for someone more exciting to get wheeled in.

By yammering on past the point when anyone cares, Margaret gets allowed to stay in the cubicle corner, offering advice and wincing on David's behalf. With rapid evolution, she becomes his agent, personal assistant, and fixer. She buttonholes tired nurses about the magic of modern dance and demands that David be made well enough to see out the rest of the season.

"Your guy here an acrobat?" a gnarly nurse shoots that at her.

"He's a very trained movement interpretist."

"I just thought he danced with his hands all the fuss you're making."

Anger swells out.

"We could go to another hospital. One that appreciates talent."

Right then, a surge of agile motion bursts through the emergency room, flapping its plastic curtains and rustling its clipboards. An onward thrust of energy, dedicated to a target. A black-clad angel, swooping to bring relief. It's Larissa Lamar. She's angry.

"Let me through. I must see David Scott."

Seeing the bed, Larissa's eyes flick to the chair in the corner. "What's that crazy doing here? She's completely mad. David. David. They let that mad woman in."

David's been given a shot of something to take off the edge. He had been enjoying a moment's respite. Something about Larissa's voice twinges his wounded bones.

"Hey, Larissa."

"Do you know how many calls I had to make? Your phone's been dead for hours. Adam and some of the company have been out looking for you. What on earth has happened? And why is that woman here?"

Funny, in this druggy state, Margaret's voice pulses a constant warm amber, but Larissa's questions flash a deep, chilly blue.

"I got into a disagreement with some guys. Just bare knuckles. Margaret helped me out."

Not asking permission, not needing to, Larissa flicks through the pictures in David's file. "Did she do this? Bind up your hand like torture? What an utterly," she turns to Margaret, "utterly stupid thing to do."

"Not really." The mumble of a tired doctor drifts past.

"She braced the fractures in place. Actually pretty sensible."

Ignoring inconvenient information, "This woman is a dangerous fantasist. She's a stalker. Come on, David. We're going home."

"Home?"

The word has special meaning, Margaret knows, when applied to two people.

"Yes."

Larissa has fabulous bones. Even hospital light can't mistake them.

"Home, where David lives. With me."

Suddenly not an agent, not an assistant, just nothing, Margaret wanders down to the street, feeling the cold where she hasn't felt it all evening. She has no clue where this hospital is. She approaches a paramedic.

"Excuse me. If you're going to the Bronx, can you give me a lift?"

6.

F rank's so old, so well set up, he can open his front door in a string vest and pajama pants and feel no way about it. Even four a.m. on a dark morning.

"Christ, you been out all night?"

"I had to take someone to hospital. Then I couldn't find a ride home. I just wandered around and got here anyway. How about I set up early?"

"You stop off on the way?"

"It was cold. I just had a couple."

Reluctantly, he lets her sit in the kitchen. Puts on coffee.

"You took someone to hospital? That it?"

"Yeah."

No point saying what's kept her walking the last couple hours. A spike of feeling makes him set a bear claw down beside her coffee.

"When you start the theater thing?"

"I'm taking a look tonight. They got doormen serving drinks—can you believe that?"

"Civilization's fallen far." He sits opposite, too old to care how he looks or smells. "If you don't mind me saying, you look like shit just now. Why not take the day off?"

In this current state, anything sounds like rejection.

"I got to be reliable for you."

"You are, believe me. You reliably sling hot milk on men's shirts, give change of a twenty on every note, and feed cats behind the wagon. I can rely on you doing all that. Why people like you. Why customers like you. You're the real deal. But today you look like you fell down a hole, so take time out. Buy a new hat."

"I could get a foam dome with coffee cups."

"I'd like nothing more."

Frank's wife walks in, a loose dressing gown and some-thing slinky beneath. She's young and has dodged all effects of pasta.

"You must be Margaret." She offers a hand. "Frank speaks so highly of you, says you're a natural on the stall."

"Phyllis," his arms fling over his head, "don't repeat what I say when I'm loaded."

Somewhat surprised, when she gets home, to find the lights and TV still on. Like somehow last night's still happening, in her apartment. It's still that moment when that nice boy from the mart closed the door. That was okay, and the ambulance ride, that too. Come on, she cajoles herself, it had to go wrong, just had to. Not just the age gap, the everything gap. And that woman, that dancer, Larissa. How anyway do you get born to a name like Larissa?

"How do people become who they are when I'm not?" The mirror has no answer for her.

She doesn't even like taking a shower because of that window. Okay, apartments, not much space, she gets it. But better a bathroom with no natural light than a window onto a staircase. Sure, it's rippled, but what's to stop anyone pressing their clammy face on it? After all, she isn't gross, she isn't done yet. Is she? Margaret pulls the shower curtain across and starts a loud conversation with two SmackDown wrestlers.

* * *

Someone else deeply unhappy that morning is the dance company's director and chief, meaning only, choreographer, a glumly nitty genius known by the single word Alpha. Born female, but beyond such things, frustratingly lacking the strength and endurance to dance, Alpha successfully strives to deliver the gorgeous, heart-quickening pains of dance onto others. Ne—Alpha's favoured gender-neutral pronoun—was one of the first to combine computer-aided dance construction with advanced mobile x-ray techniques that enabled nem to track performer's bone formations at every point of the kinsphere. There's a lot of debate on very beautiful-looking websites about Alpha.

Today, though, nirs steel-gray eyes glare with displeasure at a collection of listless bodies, some of which are hungover and one—nirs star one—has his hand swaddled in a wholly inelegant bandage.

"Who wants to go first?" demands Alpha, uncharacteristic brusqueness piquing their consciences.

"David went off-grid."

When Adam speaks aloud, he always sounds apologetic. As a gay man, he's also baffled by the sneaky attraction he feels for Alpha, like a crush on an irritable teacher.

"We were concerned. Anything could have happened. It took time to track him down."

"He was attacked," Larissa jumps in before David can speak. "In an especially urban part of the city. To make it worse, some mad woman took advantage of him. I was calling hospitals half the night."

Alpha's eyes suggest some input from David is required.

"There's nothing broken." How he says it sounds hugely defensive. "I'm grateful for everyone taking such care."

Dancers, Alpha reflects, cannot be trusted. In the cabin ne uses near Canaan, New Hampshire, ne dreams of automata sleek enough, discreet enough, to dance the dance of humans. Programmable and perfectible. Who could want more?

"Take a rest day."

Neither kind nor brutal, the voice just is.

"Be back here at four for rehearsal. David, please get a less conspicuous dressing."

Sotto voce, "You should have seen how it looked last night."

Not sotto enough. Larissa stares narrowly at him. "I need new clothes."

That bit of solidarity, bit of goodwill, when the director was present was gone now. Adam catches up with them at the door. He's a nice-looking guy, a big heart, and easy to tears. There's a bug on his shoulder now, though.

"Last night," he opens.

"Thanks, man," David squeezes his wrist. "Thanks for all you did."

"I mean our conversation. Larissa, you get a call from Berlin?"

Rolls her eyes. "Are you my mother now?"

"People are saying Pfeiffer." Desperately wanting just to stay friends. Yet this is dance and dance is everything. "That right? Pfeiffer?"

Larissa's let's-be-patient voice strips skin from bone.

"We have a huge closing night on Saturday, Adam. Let's focus on that."

"I'd rather focus on paying my rent after Saturday."

"Wouldn't we all." She makes to breeze clear.

"David, ask her. Is it Berlin?"

"Okay, man." David just wants this defused.

"We'll talk, okay?"

"Must be great," Adam says, to everyone and no one. "When you got choices."

Susan, standing silent nearby, doesn't guess she'll need to arch nearly so hard, in that off-Broadway show she just got. Everyone looks for work the whole time. Not everyone boasts what they get.

* * *

In a small, hopeless way, David thought Larissa might have been joking about new clothes, that it might have been some throwaway talk, meaning nothing. No chance.

"You've got the best eye for clothes of any straight guy I know," she tells him and off they trot to Flatiron, not even ironically. Sure, this honed and horny guy, he's tempted by the gym, the park running track, even the Donut King. But he's dutifully trailing a talented woman round the city's cooler stores, getting loaded on labels.

Meantime, Margaret is also enticed—so far as she can afford it—by retail therapy. A rough night in so many ways, and she knows she has much to prove to Letasha Wilkins, given her snow-job on the theater bar has to come real for the weekend. At least she can dress the part, in budget brands.

Bleary but barrelling-through, she hits a big store on 5th, telling the sales assistant, "I need to dress for success."

Now this young woman behind the counter, she's not a bad person. Her brother's a worry and she has her own troubles. Fatally, though, she'd rather be working furnishings than womenswear and this red-eyed baggage with the loopy lips is doing nothing to ease her day. "You want what?"

Margaret gestures up and down her body.

"Got a hot new job. Need to dress like I know."

"Know what?"

Margaret never considered before there was a comeback to that.

"I want to impress," she says confidentially, "with my class and business flair. Huh?" She gives a big wink.

"I don't know." The assistant chews her lip. "Might be a bit late for that."

Unfortunately, in the next store, Margaret encounters a properly blonde, properly steel-hard beauty. This young woman doesn't want to serve any customers, especially mumsy here, who might well be overweight beneath that baggy jacket. "I really don't think we'd have anything your size."

"You don't even know what I want."

"Whatever," the girl flicks her away with her nails. "I'm sure we don't have it."

Dejected and hiding it, how she does, Margaret totters on sleep-deprived legs south on Broadway. Whatever swampy condition she's in, she can't let the opportunity slip. "'I've been walking these streets so long, singing the same old song. I know every crack in these dirty sidewalks of Broadway.'"

Off a shot a liquor and a night at the hospital, she hits that low note fine.

Anna from *Frozen*, on her way to the Square, yells, "Quit it, you're outside the permitted zone."

Margaret turns right around to gawp. "She's put on weight." And walks backward onto the intersection.

"Hey, Dorothy." Holding his chest where he hit the steering wheel, the cop stalks from the car.

"What you doing?"

"Dorothy?" Margaret stares in his puckered, angry face.

"Oh, *Wizard of Oz*. 'Ding-dong the witch is dead...'"

"Stop. Get back on the sidewalk." The cop chivvies her out of the traffic. "You been drinking?"

"Not since the last convenience store. I been going all night."

He eyes her with the uncomfortable knowledge this won't produce any anecdotes he can be proud of.

"Do you need medical attention?" Crossing his fingers the answer's no.

"Oh no, I was at the hospital already. I bound it up in electrical tape and he was fine."

"Good. That's good."

The cop retreats to his car. "Stick to the sidewalk, okay?" He pops his head out the window. "That was the worst Munchkin I ever heard."

Bemused, Margaret tries one last clothes store.

* * *

For hours, David has followed Larissa around store after store and now has an armful of branded bags to prove it. She's buoyant, the whole Berlin thing seems to be settled, aside from the tricky issue of telling the rest of the company. It's okay, though, she reminds him—their run here ends on Saturday, she can be in Europe next week. Pfeiffer will find her somewhere to stay. Pfeiffer's psyched to get her onboard. Two years max, absolute tops, she'll engineer something for David. She paints a pretty picture and no reason at all why it shouldn't happen. Life is a cut-throat game; you take your chances.

"I just need to go in here," he says, indicating the department store. "Get some packs of socks for workouts."

"And coffee," says Larissa, feeling generous toward a good friend.

At that moment, three floors above them, Margaret is failing to make another assistant understand what she wants. It isn't that basic courtesy is alien to young people in retail, but there are so many nights and shenanigans and so little time to dissect them, and your bestie might not be on the same shift tomorrow. There's so much lingo, it changes so fast, so many verbal emojis. So much life whizzing by at li-fi speed, who knows what you miss by slowing down to comprehend some woman, old like your mom, smelling loaded like your mom, who can't explain at all what she wants to wear beyond, 'Something that looks nice'. Of course, you're going to laugh at her and make some gesture that says she's a stain. You need all the lulz you can get because, frankly, this is store work, it's lousy pay, and it sucks. While some asshole that your mom's asshole boyfriend used to hang with got swagged doing just one season of Jersey Shore.

None of this nuanced angst translates to Margaret,

who leaves feeling puffy and hurt by the whole encounter. This time, though, she gets revenge. In *Armed and Dangerous* there's that scene where Frank Dooley goes fishing. 'I got a shark, I got a shark' he yells, dragging his line down the jetty, mashing a dozen fishermen up with him. The clothes rails here are on wheels.

"I got a shark," she whispers, grabbing a rail, driving it hard against the next, locking them in a sideways hold. "I got a shark." Taking two clothes rails locked together, she sweeps them across, tangling into a third, then a fourth. A juggernaut of cheap aluminium and overpriced womenswear, slung around so another rail gets caught up, bowling over a couple of women who can't decide between blue and beige. She tips back the rails, taking out three more shoppers, one of whom lands on a hatbox and starts to scream. Nimbly—for she can move when she wants—Margaret jumps clear of the wreckage.

"Now that's fishing."

The rumpus becomes distracting enough for the staff to notice. They gesture a pair of security guys towards the disorderly scene.

"Uh-oh, SpaghettiOs." Margaret tunnels through the logjam of rails and clothes she's created, hauling with her a black pant suit off the rack. She checks the label. "My size."

At least, it will be, with a little controlled breathing.

Grabbing shirts and shrugs as camouflage, Margaret sneaks from the disaster, her good humour at a job well done short-lived. Because there, by the elevator, she sees Larissa, looking cool and dark and awesome just as she can. And there behind her is David, piled high with designer names.

As they vanish into the elevator, Margaret leaps for the stairs, doubling down two at a time, every stalking bone in her body primed for action.

* * *

Actually, this has been harder work than rehearsing modern dance. Harder because unrewarding. Larissa and David go way back—they're sometimes mistaken for lovers. David does nothing to dispel that impression— why would he? The woman is prima and headed for bigger things. This carrying clothes is donkey work, though. He hasn't even got the pack of socks he came for.

"How about that coffee?" he indicates the store café.

Earlier generosity has frayed somewhat. Larissa hates to waste time—she can't be who she is wasting time— and this has all taken way longer than she intended. She wants a soak and a massage, David's massage, before they rehearse at four. He has got a great eye, though, for cut and line, and hasn't complained at carrying her stuff.

"Just quickly," she says. "I need to get a workout."

Only the in-store café of a strip mall in California could potentially have less atmosphere than the pit stop of a big city store. Space grudgingly ceded from higher-end stock to perishables and utilitarian transaction. Even franchised out, it's never as good as the franchisee down the block.

Awkwardly fitting their beauty and grace to the most cramped of spaces, they both drink something skinny and taste-free. David suggests he might risk a small cookie, for all the energy he's expended. Larissa doubts he should. Hers is the sensible view.

Her arms alibied with unpurchased clothes, Margaret is busily scouring each floor for the gorgeous dark-dressed couple, half of whom she wishes good things to and the other half not so much. Now, of course, Margaret hasn't slept since yesterday morning. She hasn't eaten for a while—not good for someone used to pastries on tap. It's been a fraught time and she had a drink last night and now she's bone weary. Maybe it's hunger makes her see him again, that stocky, beckoning figure with the trilby hat, big overcoat, shades. Is that a cigar in his fingers? Indoors? Pointing the way to the café.

She slings the items she's carrying into a discount bin, smooths herself down and strolls ahead, trying to simulate confident poise, knocking over only one stand of accessories on the way.

In residual drunk mode, she makes the most of what the place has to offer, loading up her plate with jam doughnuts and bear claws. She says to the cash desk guy, "Coffee and a bear claw?"

He nods at her tray. He doesn't get what she wants.

"Love the darn things, I tell you," she presses on. "I can eat those things by the dozen. Fact it looks as though I have."

Sadly, he's not familiar with that scene from *Career Opportunities*.

"Yeah," he agrees, "it does look like you have."

"Listen, son." She leans over the counter. "I happen to know a great deal about the catering business. High-volume and high-end, know what I'm saying?"

He starts to feel for the panic button.

"This," she brandishes the bear claw at him, "is one of the most difficult lines to sell right. You need finesse. You need to look like your customer."

She swings around, waving the claw at his customers like a wand.

Sadly, the pastry is not of good quality and chooses that moment to split across the middle, falling to the floor. Rapidly losing balance on her tray of doughnuts and coffee, she rams the truncated end of claw into her mouth, to free her hand to stop the tray falling.

At that moment, David's gaze moves from Larissa—so lithe and untainted by crumbs—to this dishevelled, insane-looking woman with half a pastry lodged in her mouth, on which she's now choking. The decision made in his body before it reaches his brain, David jumps up and runs to her, taking in her bulging eyes, her surprisingly cute little ears, and the large mouth fitfully heaving at pastry.

Moving behind, he gets his arms around her tender belly and squeezes hard.

With rocket force, the half claw launches from her lips, sailing in a graceful arc, gently showering crumbs before crash-landing at Larissa's feet.

"Oh shit," bellows Margaret, tumbling forward, clinging to her coffee tray like a clown in a balance act.

She pulls David—who forgot to let go—along with her. He lunges down, grabbing at his bound-up hand. "Oh shit," clasping hold of it as he falls.

Margaret, still on her feet, gradually pivots round. "David," she shouts delightedly, "what a lovely surprise."

Gathering her shopping bags, Larissa sails past, booting pastry debris across the room.

"David." Her voice travels behind her. "Let's go."

7.

Letasha Wilkins has all the stories: university of life, school of hard knocks, blah blah. Her brothers still out there, doing shit, wondering why they get busted for it. She'd love to do outreach, like that teacher she had in jail, but it doesn't put asses on seats.

Still, in a small way, she feels she's helped the community. She's taken on this woman, who clearly has issues, to remodel the theater café. Though as 'taken on' actually means a free trial, maybe it's not such a great act of altruism to pitch to the trustees.

The woman has made an effort, no doubt. She seems to have washed her face and hair. She's almost free of food crumbs. And black stretch jeans and an old Ramones tee are not wholly off the vibe. As Margaret rejigs chairs and tables, setting up potted plants she's cadged off market stalls, arranging bottles of obscure Italian liqueurs on the shelf, hammering nails into the partition walls not quite strong enough to hang pictures, the black clad young doormen move defensively round her, seeming concerned she might contaminate them somehow.

"How's it going?" Letasha isn't quite sure why she finds the leopard print rug so especially disturbing.

Margaret, who sweats disarmingly freely, flings a Coney Island smile. "Great, Tasha."

No one here calls her Tasha.

"Really great. If we could just get rid of this wall, we could open right out some."

"Then you'd be in the auditorium."

Stern Ms. Wilkins can't resist a smile.

"Oh that would be so cool." That agile, never-still face fills with wonder. "We could have the bar at the back, for slow bits when people get bored."

"I'll mention it to the artistic director." Letasha squints at near-illegible script on the chalkboard. "What are your specials?"

"We got amaretto and honeycomb, and Kir frappe—fresh and alcoholic!"

"Any coffee?"

"When I get the blender to work, there's a Kit Kat Frappuccino."

"You're very creative."

"Shucks." Margaret scuffs her shoes. "I just spend a lot of time alone."

* * *

In a different field of the performing arts, rehearsals are somewhat soured by the atmosphere that's taken hold lately. Dance is a close, tight world—no way to do this otherwise. It's trust and respect, empathy, back-breaking work. So when you're breaking your back for minimum rate and you know that one of your brightest colleagues doesn't care so much anymore, because she has a sweet job elsewhere—a job you might want a crack at—even the toughest pro gets focus issues.

For Alpha, it just proves nirs theory that humans are the least-equipped for rigorous physical expression. For David, it's acutely uncomfortable. He's a sensitive guy, he feels trouble brewing, he wants—in an old-school way—everyone to just get along. He's also conscious that, when Larissa gets on that plane, he still needs to work with the people she's pissed off, and all the other people who've been told about it. With everyone fishing in the same pool, make no mistake, Larissa has torched her bridges in truly Wagnerian fashion, leaving David as her severed limb, still showing for Monday's auditions.

It boils up when Susan, troubled, sometimes awkward, flubs a transfer and breaks the flow of the piece.

Icy Alpha stares. Larissa kicks off. "What do you think you're doing? We've danced this a hundred times. It's not a surprise to you, surely. Don't you practice?"

"Practice?" Slight, ephemeral Susan gathers breath. "I do nothing but practice. You've seen my feet."

"Oh please," Larissa waves, "we all have cuts."

"I got a cramp." Susan clutches her leg.

"Then warm up."

"I do warm up. I'm doing my best to get this right. Some of us have to work at it." That's emotive, everyone works at it.

David dips a toe in. "Larissa didn't mean harm. It's just the moment."

"What?" Larissa steams around on him. "Are you my interpreter now? You tell people what I mean?"

"Won't need an interpreter in Berlin, will you, darling?" Adam, from the darkness. "You can say all you mean with your ass."

Ungracefully, she snaps, "It couldn't be as busy as yours."

Slowly, with great finesse, Adam draws his hand downwards, miming a claw. In a tight, strangled pantomime tone, "Me-owwww."

"Enough." For once, even Alpha has to control nir breathing. "Enough. We are performing tonight, if I can just trouble you with that information. You have two hours. Then back here ready." Time for nem to Skype a certain German choreographer about reparations.

Larissa, pissed not to get the last word, looks round the stage with open annoyance. "You don't have what it takes. You just don't."

She sweeps her superstar self through the black painted doors into the lobby.

"Would you like to try my Scotch whisky brûlée?"

It's the very worst nightmare. A broken, failed rehearsal, sudden, unflattering light, and a lunatic foisting high calorie gunk.

"Would I what?"

"Puts a spring in your spring!" Margaret mashes a spoon around the strange auburn gloop.

"Wherever I turn you are there." Larissa's heart rate doubles. "Wherever I go, whatever I do, I see your stupid grinning face, your rat hair, your ugly breasts…"

"Ugly?"

"And destroying things with your out-of-control, untrainable body. And eating. And talking this strange fucking language. I hope you drown in brûlée. I hope you fall in a great big tub of it and sink right out of my life."

There are tears, Margaret sees them. On Larissa's fine cheeks are tears. A woman as in need of a hug and a bear claw as any that Margaret has seen, in her twelve-hour days tending to the hungry and lost at an East Village intersection. But what can you do? What help can you give if someone locks themselves in their own bubble? Heave a shrug and walk away. What anyone would do. Except Margaret Rudge. She stows the brûlée that will never be cleaned from the bowl and chases out after Larissa.

Late summer warmth has already shrunk away from these fall afternoons. Evening, nearly, the oblong sky between blocks dirtying with night. Margaret beetles down Rivington. Literate in sadness she knows exactly where someone poised and careful like Larissa would go. Deep misery needs an expansive stage, someplace huge and dramatic. The shadows between the towers at Columbia Street.

In this, Margaret's instinct is flawless. There's Larissa beneath the shedding trees, quietly fabulous under Baruch Houses. A piece of theater perfected in bruised human form. Margaret hasn't seen Larissa alone and motionless before, and marvels how every part of her lives in exact accord with every other. But this is no black-painted performance space. The street is Margaret's stage, which Larissa understands, so ice sets hard in her gaze.

"Go ahead. Take a picture. It's what you want, isn't it? It must be wonderful, being such a saint. They should name a corner for you. One of those scratty asphalt slicks where drunks throw up."

Margaret stays carefully out of arm's reach.

"I think we got off on the wrong foot. I don't want anything bad for you."

"Well, there." Larissa looks away, hiding her tear stains in shadows. "Keep proving you're saintly."

"Not at all." Gently as she can, Margaret perches on the bench. "When I blend a drink or something, I just want people to like it and think I might be good at something. I'm really small in the scheme of things. It's real folks, like David and you, who have talent."

Larissa makes a big, obvious huff.

"I don't want sisterly crap. I want the admiration of my betters."

"So do I."

"Would you do me a huge favour?"

Okay, the tone is regal snark, but Margaret's game enough to say, "Sure."

With swift precision, Larissa turns to face her. "Stop pretending."

"What?"

"Stop pretending you're dumb. Stop pretending you don't have ambition." The venom's there and, distilled, strategically twines through Larissa's patrician vowels. "You wheedle your way in everywhere, you make everyone do what you want. You sweat on people, they love you for it. Why work for admiration when you can put Skittles through a blender?"

"I know you work hard." Fleetingly, Margaret wonders if the pain is some new bruise or an old one revisited. "I've seen you work. You'll always be best."

"No I won't."

"Okay, you get older."

Shocking, almost, that slender, muscular grip on Margaret's pudgy forearm.

"I went to pre-class when I was four years old. I started ballet at eight. My parents are rich, of course, but that's not always enough. I was the striving one, the busy one, hungry for improvement. I did nothing but practice. I wasn't the best in class. There was another girl. Her mother worked three jobs to keep her at ballet school. That girl, Christine, was fluid, precise. She could tie her fucking bun better than me."

"That matters?"

"Everything matters. I so wanted to be better than her. Then when she was eleven she started to grow."

Perplexed, Margaret looks at the woman beside her.

"Yeah, you're pretty tall."

Anger hardens the grip on Margaret's arm. "I said stop acting dumb. Christine started to grow her chest. Training reduces body fat, but, regardless, her breasts grew huge and ugly. You can't dance with mounds of fat. Her mother couldn't afford reduction surgery. I laughed when Christine left in tears. I was top of the class."

"You laughed?"

"You're judging me. Fine. I'm used to it." Larissa stands, hands on hips, smoothing back her dress to sketch her shape. "I was an adolescent girl, scared to death the same would happen to me. I got a roll of tape and strapped mine down. I still do."

Puzzled, but aware this is more than boasting, Margaret asks, "What happened to Christine?"

Larissa sweeps her arms to a Spanish fourth. "Dance was her life. She hung herself. With a scarf that looked like silk but was nylon. She was fourteen years old. My career should have been hers. It's a street fighting business. Why don't you go make some brûlée?"

Margaret hurries back to the theater. What she needs is there. Larissa went off to walk to the river leaving Margaret making silent wishes that no harm should come to that beautifully-managed form.

"She can be number one," Margaret tells the sidewalk and the sidewalk believes her.

David, bored with stretching while trying to rest his arm, surveys from a safe distance the gunk on the bar counter. He feels a lift to the air when Margaret arrives. "What's that?"

"I got the blender to work."

"We thought someone was drilling the road."

"Maybe it needs a muffler or something."

He watches her fuss ineffectually at the blender. "I got an hour till show time. Want to grab some food?"

"Can you dance on food?"

"On spinach, yeah, but eggplants get too slippy."

That grin—how does anyone grin that way?

"I'll just get changed."

* * *

Now just to rewind that, Margaret lives the other end of the island and is hardly the type to carry a change of clothes. So, while David heads off to get them a booth in this sweet little retro diner, she's skittering over 1st Avenue, tearing up the sidewalk to reach the Thrift Boutique.

Japanese girls hanging by the window, pointing and giggling at the old gowns, step back and some cower a little as this mighty bolt of Ramones and stretch dodges the traffic shouting cusses and smacks against the front door. A brief interlude of birds singing round her head, she fixes up and goes inside.

"Angelica, you got to help me."

The woman in vintage Lauren steps back.

"I'm Agatha."

"Sorry." Darn twins.

"Agatha, I need a going-out dress."

"When you going out?"

"Already." Impatiently, Margaret starts flicking the racks of pre-loved material.

"How 'bout this?" then chokes at the price tag.

"It's Dior, silly."

"Sheesh, how much was it new?"

"Less than that. You have a price in mind?"

"Agatha." The woman flinches bodily. "I got a date with a guy, like, sixteen years younger. You got to help me."

"What's he do, this guy?"

"Dances ballet." Margaret attempts a wide fourth, knocking over some hats.

The co-proprietrix of this cavern of silky delights looks a tad skeptical. "For real?"

"Look at me. Would I joke about something like that? He's in the diner now."

"Back here." Agatha gestures. "Try this red baby."

"It's awfully flared."

"It's a Lindy hop dress. Totally timeless."

Margaret clamps it against her. "Doesn't touch my knees."

"You'd rather your knees were a shock to him later?"

* * *

Forty minutes of the hour left. David has downed two mineral waters and is starting to feel self-conscious. Strikes him he hardly ever goes out on his own, eating alone. Always in a gang of guys, energizing on a cellular level. Or with the whole company, shaking the vodka tree, or with Larissa. Almost never he goes out with any woman but Larissa. He doesn't want to hurt her, even though he knows she's going to be hurt. They've had enough time, haven't they? Nothing's happened to now.

All around, people on creepy diets and people who don't give a shit stoke up on whatever the menu has to offer. He chose this place consciously thinking it might appeal to her, that she might find it fun. Larissa wouldn't find it fun. Why should that matter?

Again, he puts off the waitress. She's given him that waitress sympathy look. She thinks he's been stood up.

An almighty clatter by the front door, someone shouts, a general commotion that he doesn't need to turn around to interpret. Something weird happens inside David's chest. His heart picks up the beat.

"Sorry I been so long. There was a line for the ladies' room." So out of breath she can hardly stand, flushed and glowing—so obvious she's been running. She smacks her hair back down with her palms. Wearing an old red dress with half a mile of twirling skirt. Her other clothes, the clothes she was wearing twenty minutes ago, punched into a thrift store bag. Her knees and lower legs tell the story of many journeys to the ground.

"You look awesome," he says. She does.

"Aw." She flicks round the hem. "It's some old lady's dress. They got out nearly all the stains." She collapses into the booth, lightly head-butting the gent sitting behind. He jolts forward, jabbing at his ears.

"What you like to eat? They got pancakes."

"I got to dance tonight." Where's this voice come from? Is it his voice?

"Oh, baby. I mean." Horror engulfs her face. "David. I said 'Oh, David'. Always working so hard."

"Doesn't Margaret's Barre open tonight?"

"Silly, I'm not calling it that. Though I could get a twisty green neon sign." She squiggles it with her finger.

Back comes the waitress. "You two here for the scenery?"

"What can you eat?" A hands-clasped leer of concern, like talking to an invalid.

David can't even begin with the menu. "You got soup?"

"Minestrone or chicken."

"Oh," Margaret's mouth gapes. "I love minestrone, so artisan."

"Two please." David grins.

Beneath her thick lipstick, the waitress is fighting a smile.

"I'll miss this town," David says, just meaning conversation.

"You going away?" Margaret slumps.

"The season ends Saturday. Some of the guys have got a job in Canada. Might go with them. Maybe get a week on chorus in Vancouver."

"Chorus?" Her horrified voice fills the rafters. "You're a star."

That makes him chuckle.

"I'm a guy who feels too much of his spine in the morning. I'm pushing it, you know. Twenty-five. If I'm not a big someone three years from now, game over."

"That's silly," she snortles. "Age is just a number. I'm thirty-five and six years, and my energy levels are still super high. Fact, I'm frustrated as hell." The mouth stays open, but all sound stops. Tentatively, she asks, "Do I come off a tad pushy?"

He throws back his head, gives his teeth some air. "No. Not at all."

The waitress lays down the plates, tells them to enjoy.

"Shall I eat your bread?" Margaret offers. "So you don't get bulimic."

Between them they scrape enough change for the check.

"One course is fine," she assures him. "I have dessert at home. Where we're not going, I mean."

"I got to go plié."

As they walk back to the theater, the sun's sinking down and a brash little chill is picking up from the East River. There might be cocktails going on in a waterfront condo on some more presented shore. But across the drink in Green and Dupont and all the other streets, most folks are cracking beer, watching TV, not thinking of the shit they do for money. Doesn't occur to Margaret, in her prickly, red-dress excitement, how different and more exquisite life has become.

Sensing the time's been short, David offers, "We could meet up, when there's longer, you know. Maybe go to a movie."

"I'm not sitting through *Hedwig and the Angry Inch* again."

He ponders this. "You don't have to."

"Thought it was a comedy."

"It is a comedy."

"I thought: head, wig, inch. Writes itself."

"Friend of mine danced the show. The tour production."

"Gee, guess you gotta do whatever." In a slot of dark, she says, "May I ask you a question?"

Anything could be coming. David doesn't mind.

"When I was out today, just doing stuff," she begins carefully, "someone said I have ugly breasts. Do you have a view on that?"

"Ugly?"

"My breasts. Are they ugly?"

"No." Who the hell said that? He wants to give them a taste of his good hand. "You have good breasts. Really, noticeably good."

"I'm actually clenching my shoulders so hard it hurts."

They kind of touch hands and it feels like a warm human hand is meant to feel.

* * *

There's a dance show, but Margaret doesn't see it. Surprisingly many of the hip and enlightened warm to the notion of Kir frappe and a few don't actually make it as far as the black painted doors. There's a persistent slick of custard on the floor, which provides some excitement, and a couple of the doormen sacrifice their black shirts to the cause of blended drinks. Margaret, in her swing time dress, presides over a riot of incorrect change that sees the house marginally up at the end of the night.

Once the last sugar junkie has been helped outside,

she waits hopefully for the dancers, but they vanished through the stage door, less than usually buoyant, talking in low voices, their gang cutting into cliques, leaving Larissa and David alone.

As Margaret tries to dismantle her blender, Letasha Wilkins appears from her office. Always austere in something tight and black, she looks more than ever distracted.

"I hear the bar went well."

"They were very enthusiastic." Margaret is pulling nougat from the rotor blades. "I'll get a ladder tomorrow, peel that taffy off the ceiling. Who'd have thought salt water would stick like that?"

"Sheridan Ringley's here tomorrow for the season close."

"Ringley?" Margaret studies the treacly gunk in her hands. "Why's that name...? Ringley? The circus guy?"

"Her ancestor. From circuses to Broadway to she owns this block. Thinks we should be more popular."

"That's silly. You're sold out every night."

"To the same people. That's the issue. To the same slender, misguided demographic that thinks modern dance means something." Ms. Wilkins takes a shot from an unlabelled bottle. "What in Christ is this?"

"My own recipe ginger mixer."

"I can't feel my throat."

"It's two parts rectified spirit. I never have a cold."

Ms. Wilkins takes another shot. "Ms. Sheridan Ringley has turned twenty-five, which means she knows everything. If we can't show we have a plan to broaden participation here, I'm sure she'll find something more lucrative to do with her inheritance."

"Money," Margaret sighs. "Sure doesn't make folks happy. Except for my ex and my boss."

* * *

Prophetic words from someone who's lived a little. Walking eight blocks to catch her bus home, her phone rings and Margaret is jam-brained excited, thinking it might be David. Then she remembers—he doesn't have her number.

Early evening in Phoenix, the sun not yet down. Shouting receding behind, like someone walking briskly from a car smash. "Hey princess!" So this is Tommy. Tommy who went to court to make her stop calling. "Been a while, babe, how swings it?"

Instinctively, she checks around, in doorways, over her shoulder, to see if this is a prank.

"That you Tommy?"

"The very actual." Definite, some kind of rumpus, and him moving fast, she can hear his change jingle. What's going on in Phoenix? "Bet it's oh-so cold out East."

"Possibly. I don't know. I'm wearing a coat." She's wearing a T-shirt over a dress over stretch jeans.

"Keeping busy Princess?"

"Tommy, are you on drugs? You never called me Princess. Is this a wrong number, do you think you've found your girlfriend?"

Heavy, wholly expected pause. "This is a right number. I been thinking, babe. I got business out east in a couple of weeks. Maybe you and me could hook up, dust off the old-times'-sake."

She stands at an intersection. Young people bubble around her. Guatemalan food, Mongolian food—the whole world right on her taste buds. It's not strange anymore being here on her own. She has work here.

"What about your shrink? She alright with something for the sweet tooth?"

"Juliette? She got kind of angry last night. The police here are rather a brash bunch. They suggested I might take some time."

"Out of Phoenix?"

"Outside the Mountain Time Zone. Thing is, Margaret," he lays heavy chops on her name. "Thing is, you see, Juliette, she's just not you."

What a chance, a two-footed leap in the dark straight down a crap hole.

"She's not me, that what you're saying Tommy?" There's her bus, limbering for the crawl at the next intersection. "That's it? Juliette, she's not me?"

"She's not you, babe."

"So now you know, douchebag, what it's like with someone not me." She kills the call, points gun fingers at her phone. "Shot down."

Far end of the ride, that little warm cockle of victory fades—she's squeamish about seeing Bobby. She understands there's this thing, where two lonely people in the same street get it on. She wonders she might still need that, once Sunday comes and the dance leaves town. But for now, it doesn't seem right, getting groceries, talking groceries, letting him treat her to chocolate, which he surely pays for. Not an ounce of guile nor bad heart sullies her body. She doesn't scheme and set up substitute dates for when the real love falls through. That's why she's alone.

So, although she could do with this and that, and thread where her socks need mending, she doesn't walk down to the Moonlight Supermart. She enters her building, like always making as much noise as she can, pretending like always that she's about three different people. Then she sits on her couch, not getting the gags on the late show, wishing she had gone to the store, wishing somehow to rewind the last twenty-four hours.

"Beam me up Scotty," she calls to the fractured ceiling, knowing that phrase was never spoken, not in any episode or film, and Scotty's ashes barely left Earth at all.

Down the street, Bobby's busy night runs the same as always—the hookers and drunks, a tearful runaway picked up by the cops. She keeps pleading with them not to tell her mom, like they won't do that. Inbetween times, Bobby watches the door, a bag of jellybeans paid for under the counter.

8.

Sheridan Ringley already left Columbus. Less than two hours direct, but a couple of people with her need sightseeing time. Insanely hyped on their first trip to New York. Clyde Demaria got her to do this trip. Sheridan prefers keeping tabs on her empire remotely, she likes the climate in Columbus and, walking by the rivers, feels a certain vacant gratitude for her good fortune in owning half the town. At twenty-five she's fixed on the notion of being a recluse, being someone people come to see—well-informed, but invisible to them. Like the Mighty Oz, but properly powerful.

Clyde Demaria, as a straight, reliable attorney, advised her that when there's bad news to share, face to face is best. His own double life gives him a keen appreciation of the power of publicity. He reminds her what a big figure her ancestor cut on Broadway, like that could have any meaning to her. Sheridan just likes being alone, with this same couple of people. She had a bower built in her garden, where she can't be seen, not even by drone. She thinks sometimes about not existing at all, about how that would feel. She's come very close. She has no fear.

Clyde Demaria, as a sensible business adviser, tells her to visit Letasha Wilkins, to do it early, well before tonight's grand show. Sheridan checks online details of the program, regards the gloomy pictures of human bodies bent and shaped to near-impossible ends. Bones tell stories—the phrase disturbs her. Look how their bones erupt from their skin. What celebration is this. Sheridan Ringley escaped being bullied at school by having warring parents who were both fantastically wealthy. She had a bodyguard in case she got kidnapped. She has disturbing dreams of waves crashing on a dark beach, on a coast she doesn't recognize. She wakes sweating and times her heart at 125 beats per minute. Sheridan Ringley is coming to town.

* * *

On the inside of her wall cupboard, Letasha hung a mirror. Not wanting to get called out as vain, and also wanting to project the impression of constant, effortless, elegant drive, she only checks the mirror with her office door locked. Performing arts are a late-night business. In daytimes, nothing gets done before noon, except for that crazy woman rocket-bombing the lobby with alcoholic smoothies. Performances start late, end later. Dinner is midnight, more like one a.m. There are parties, after-parties, deliciously predatory men on the doorstep at times of the night the moon would blush to see. It's swell, at airports, to tell cubicle spackle, "Oh, I work in the arts." It's hell on the skin, though. And the pocketbook. And she needs some bajillionaire to fly in to tell her: work harder. She works a little more cream in the dents beneath her eyes that, inexplicably, only ever get deeper.

A courtesy call from Clyde says they're on their way.

She teases flat her expensively-straightened hair. Her mom had supremely sexy hair, called it afro, in the manner of the old days. She never took shit from anyone, with that monument of hair.

There's a knock and Letasha hustles to unlock the door. Clyde Demaria pushes it wider, simultaneously checking the soles of his patent shoes. He admits a slight, sunless young woman, whose lank, side parted brown hair keeps dipping across her right eye. In her plain white shirt and blue chinos she could be a subway ticket inspector, a waitress, or any young woman on the road to flunking out. Her brown eyes scan the room like taking pictures. She stares momentarily at Letasha, before offering an uninterested hand.

"Sheridan Ringley. Why do you have newspaper stuck to the floor of your lobby?"

"It's our new destination café-bar. I think there are teething problems with the equipment. Can I get you coffee?"

"A rather lively woman tried to give me what she called a Baileys Luxe."

"She's," Letasha modulates her voice, "on a program."

"Mr. Demaria got some of it on his shoes. Can I sit down? Walking fatigues me."

Edgewater fly-girl, Letasha knows this for an act. No one frail gets to have trillions of dollars. It's cozy with three of them in the small office. Letasha sits back from her desk, Clyde perches on a corner stool, and Sheridan— though wispy—seems to take most of the space.

In the manner of business, she says, "I'll come right

to the point. I'm very admiring of your work here and of course I'm very keen to support the arts."

"It's deductible," offers Letasha.

"It is, though that doesn't bother me." She clasps her hands on the desk. Their veins make the fingers nearly blue.

"My forebear, who bought this property and created the endowment, made his fortune in popular entertainment. Some of which," she's well-prepared, "may not accord with our standards today, but which, of its time, was popular."

"He gave opportunities to overlooked people." Clyde nods agreement with himself.

"Excellence is no bad thing. Neither is entertainment. Excellence and entertainment do not cancel each other out. Do you host much street dance here?"

"The street does." Letasha won't have 'the street' card played on her.

"Do you have a program for schools or links with cor-rectional services?"

This barely-audible voice, reciting the language of costly, liberal things. Letasha takes hold on the underside of her desk to avoid easily-misunderstood body language. "Typically, those services have little money to support arts outreach. The trustees are very active in raising funding, but sustained engagement requires long-term resources. I'm sure the trustees would be open to a conversation."

"I've spoken with them."

"You have?"

"They're old and white and like things how they are." She

has no expression, this woman. Her hands only unclench to lift the hair from her right eye.

"I've asked Mr. Demaria to instigate their removal."

"Ms. Ringley." Don't lose it, Letasha, don't lose it. "You own the ground on which this building stands. You control the endowment. You don't have a casting vote on the trustees."

"I do, Ms. Wilkins. I control the endowment."

"So you're going to invest?"

"I have to ensure that the money is sustainably managed. It's all I have."

Whether her life is long or short, Sheridan intends spending the rest of it in her bower.

"I'm happy to consider proposals around facilities, equipment, alternate performance spaces, so forth. But I need from you, as manager, a sustainable business plan, for audience diversification and engagement with the community beyond the tight fitting ironic T-shirts of the East Village."

"You want me go mainstream?"

"People flocked to musicals during the Depression. Not all of them lived on Park Avenue. Personally, Ms. Wilkins, I like showbiz. I look forward to receiving your plans next week. New appointments will be made to the trust board shortly."

"And if we can't shift the box office?"

As she stands, Sheridan holds her floppy hair clear of her face.

"Then this street gets some new affordable housing. Good day, Ms. Wilkins."

Clyde tilts forward off the stool. The soles of his shoes stick to the floor and he bounces back and forth like Judge Doom, before peevishly pulling his legs up from his shoulders.

Letasha thinks Sheridan is white trash, then says a quick prayer of repentance. But the thought can't be un-thought.

* * *

What a gala affair this last night is. The doomed trustees are back, though some—including Gerry—are secretly glad to be rid of this white elephant obligation. He's also rid of Cindy. Not personal, just a younger model who's even more creative in his sub-basement.

While Cindy stays home, scouring Craigslist for oblig-ing older men, she misses Margaret's grand debut as pa-tronne of the theater bar at season finale.

Sensitive to the occasion, Margaret has been to the costume hire store and is decked out in a tux, white shirt, and bowtie that would have looked no worse on the late Michael Jackson. Pre-emptively, she's done a deal to get the place cleaned up for tomorrow. Buzzy on Kit Kat Frappuccino or rendered into a vegetative state by ginger mixer, the festive crowd packs the lobby, spilling out onto the sidewalk. It's all very clubby and friendly and sweet—really, really sweet—but the nag, nag, nag in Letasha's brain is these people all know each other. They've seen this program before, some bulk-bought tick-ets even before the Buy button on the website went public. These are her people, she loves them. But Sheridan Ringley, in a man's shirt and black slacks, surrounded by minders, does not.

Margaret wants to go backstage and wish luck to the dancers. She's even bought David a present—a pack of thick socks for winter workouts. But there's a lot of business coming her way and she understands clearly that going backstage, seeing Larissa, taking those scowls and cutting remarks would hurt her more than the pleasure that seeing David brings. It's a delicate balance, this making your way through the treacherous fields of life.

Bells start to ring and the crowd hustles in, excited, delighted at all the experiences their life-choices have brought them. Letasha thinks she should accompany Sheridan Ringley to some VIP seating roped off by the stage, but the young woman seems in no hurry to move. Her loss. What's the good of having all that cash anyway?

The music begins, the black-shirt doormen shush the black doors shut. The last stragglers stumble in. Sheridan Ringley dismisses her bodyguards to go smoke.

She approaches the woman in the tux, who is counting and recounting quite a pile of money, as though both counting and money are unfamiliar and troublesome to her. The floor is sticky, despite various cloths that have been thrown down during the pre-show scrum.

"Hello," says Sheridan in her quiet voice. "You run the bar concession?"

"Margaret Rudge. You want rum fudge?"

She sees a pleasant enough young woman, who could

perhaps be improved with a better skin routine and brushing back her hair.

"Ah," says Sheridan, holding back that hair. "It's a play on your name."

Margaret trips a little on that dissection of her line.

"You're missing the show."

"I've seen video of it. They're extremely accomplished."

"Yeah, the male principal, he's a dish." Wholly genuinely, Margaret shudders with pleasure.

Cautious not to stick to anything, Sheridan carefully picks at bottles.

"Do all these drinks have an element of danger?"

What does this strange creature want? Margaret tries peeling a ten that's got stuck to her palm. She tries with her teeth.

"Fun. I prefer to say they're fun drinks."

"Bought with fun coupons." Sheridan folds a hundred into the cash drawer.

"You didn't take a drink."

"So?" She looks around. "What do you think of the audience here?"

There's a seriousness to the question, more danger than fun. Margaret steps wary. "I think these dancers need an audience. They're artists, performers."

"I watched you work this bar. You're a performer."

"Yeah, but they're good at something it's worth being good at. That makes them artists. They need an audience and this is the audience they have."

"What about street kids, in-between kids. What about

everyone who never gets the opportunity to be moved by the power of dance?"

"I don't know." Margaret navigates one of her own concoctions. "Me, I never was moved by it. Then I got to know David."

"Your boyfriend?"

"Aw, don't say that." Margaret's shoulders do the wriggle. "But once I got to know him, I got to know his dance. I can't love it as much as he does, but I can see why it's loved. How about you?"

"In property holdings, investments, and cash I'm worth about a trillion dollars. I don't need to like anything."

That can't be right. Margaret shakes her sugary hair.

"Doesn't it make you crazy having all that money?"

"I dropped out of school when I was fourteen. Ran with gangs, did a lot of meth. Had my daughter when I was fifteen, had my son the year after. If you want to be blunt and to the point, you could say I was a meth whore. Not that you could say it. My lawyers would silence your ass from here to eternity if you took any of that online. My children are at my hotel on Park Avenue. The hotel my family owns. If the nanny has done her job, they should be sleeping, though I doubt it. They're probably watching TV." She holds back hair from her flat, brown eyes. "I don't think it's good enough to say all I did is by-gones. Some people like drugs, they want drugs, it's a free market. But I think some people might want modern dance, if they just had chance to see it. But all you have in that room next door is the usual faces. Great artists, killing their backs for the usual faces. Do you think that's good enough Ms. Rudge?"

"I'm really not political. I like entertainment."

"Exactly. Leaving aside your friend next door, would you rather watch dance or *Scooby Doo?*"

"TV episode, TV movie, or live action?"

"Do you have any normal drinks here?"

"None at all."

First time since she left her kids at the hotel, Sheridan permits a small smile. She keeps them rationed, knowing she'll run dry one day.

"I think Ms. Wilkins will take some persuading that I'm right."

"There's funds though." Margaret scratches her head, surprised that some Skittles seem to be stuck there. "Charitable this and that. Stuff for underrepresented colours, diverse genders. The police have funding for programs, if you can get them to admit it. Ms. Wilkins, she knows all that. She's smart. But she's got no one to chase it up for her."

"I think Ms. Wilkins perceives an uphill struggle."

"All it takes is a bit of hustle. Bit of soft sell and hard sell. My ex-husband, he sold Hondas, so he had technique."

Margaret remembers what Tommy used to say. "It's the hot button. That money's just there to be spent. You got to hit the hot button to get it. Sometimes, all it takes is coffee and a bear claw."

"John Candy."

"You know it?" Margaret goggles at this near-translucent female.

Sheridan makes finger quote-marks: "'Melanoma head.'"

"Gee, you're cool."

Sheridan shakes her head; her hair falls half across her face.

"I still need a fix sometimes. I hide from my children that sometimes I head downtown for ice pills. Two or three times a year, still. When I'm wretched and empty. I often think of death. I sometimes think dead's better."

"*Pet Sematary*. Said by Fred Gwynne."

"Herman Munster. You see a lot of TV in meth houses."

"What about your kids, though?"

"I'm not sweet enough for the Yellow Brick Road, Ms. Rudge. It takes someone far more caring."

* * *

Always that disconnect, huh? Between the vision under the spotlights and the dirtiness backstage. The show is a smash, of course, the season finale. They even dance an encore. Some piece of whimsy to leave the customers beaming. There's no business like show business.

Backstage, though, with the sounds of the crowd filtering out, with the small disasters caused by Margaret's experiments subsiding, there's no triumphant talk from the company, no raucous late supper and drinks. Sick of the snide innuendo, Larissa lays down her resignation and gets a mouthful off Susan as buried animosities stumble out.

There's accusations of this and that and, weirdly, though Larissa has broken the troupe in two, it's David who picks up her static. She's too supreme, too bound to succeed, too likely to be necessary in some conceivable future, to really piss her off the way people want to. So, they go for David, who's been her housemate and chief cheerleader so long. The dancers leave in ones and twos, timing exits like the pros they are, so they won't have to walk up the street with each other.

Margaret waits in the lobby with a big grin and an outstretched pack of socks. Larissa barges through, pausing just fractionally long enough to appraise her. "You look pretty fucking silly standing like that." Then, more pertinently from the door, "You won't have him, you know. He's just being nice. He's being charitable to the hopeless. Why would he want you? Ask yourself. Stop being a fool."

When David comes through a few minutes later, it takes all Margaret has—which is a lot—to retrieve that grin.

"I got you a present. Socks!"

David's tired of it all. This town, the repertoire, how it was all good and it went sour so fully, so fast. He doesn't want to go back and pack his bag alongside a silent Larissa. He just wants time and space and air, alone. But he's a nice guy, and this sweet woman bought him socks.

"Thank you," he takes them, like plucking something from an automatic grab hand. "They're just my size."

"They're special nylon. Hard-wearing."

"I got a train first thing tomorrow."

"You want to do dinner?"

"Better not."

Only later, when it's just her and the janitor left in the building, does Margaret go down to the change room, looking for some trace of David, some final taste of his scent. Something tickles her nose and she drops to the floor, purposefully this time. There's the shrivelled-up bear claw, right from the first day, mouldering under the bench.

"You don't want one and I don't need one." She stays on all fours, crying, till the janitor turns off the lights. Then she cries in the dark.

9.

There's always this post-orgasmic chill after a season. The next morning, when the theater's dark and maintenance gets done, and the manager—if she has nothing already—starts calling around for the next show. Anyone travelling through who can do a one-nighter. It's that kind of trade.

"Margaret. I didn't realize we were already a destination café."

"Oh, I'm not setting up today, Letasha. I'm with Frank on East 7th. I just wanted to run something by you." Sales talk. She's been brushing the lingo all night. Pretty much she never sleeps now.

"Go on." Letasha leans back in her chair. "I find my diary surprisingly light today."

"Hey, cool." Margaret parks herself in sales pose, all business on the guest chair. "I was speaking with that Ms. Ringley last night."

"God, what did you say to her?"

"She's a most perplexing young woman." That ludicrous, room-filling whisper. "I think she has issues."

"I'm sure that's not for us to discuss."

"We weren't talking about that anyway." Margaret's toes are firmly crossed. "We were talking about her plans for this place. All the broadening out, so forth."

"I told her." Letasha shakes her fine hair. "I can't afford the time and resource of going through every possible avenue of funding. I'm here on my own. Besides, the trustees brought adequate sponsorship from their business interests. She fired the trustees, did you hear that? Now there'll be induction meetings, budget meetings— we had things running okay. Now it's a scramble."

"That's what she's saying. There's a heap of funding if you do the hustle." Van McCoy's greatest hit fills her head. She crossly shakes it out. "When my ex-boss ran off with all that money, I spent hours with the police going through the accounts. They even had me figured as an accessory. For a time."

"You paid your debt to society."

"Oh no. Anyway, I got lots of contacts in the police. There's all kinds of program funding, but it takes tenacity to find it. I could supply that tenacity."

"You can write grant applications?"

"Didn't know I could make a latte, till I ruined a few pairs of pants. And the bar killed it last night, we made enough to pay for the liquor."

"You didn't pay for it upfront?"

"I'm kind of okay at getting people to cut deals."

"I can't pay you."

"I'm used to that. I get a cut off Frank and I got a bounty hunter sitting on my ex for alimony. All his clothes are alligator skin."

"The bounty hunter?"

"I don't think Tommy would sell many Hondas in alligator skin. Not even in Phoenix."

It's starting to look attractive. Someone to do the grunt work. Someone who seems to like it. Letasha beams. "Then we have a deal."

"Oh," Margaret's best Columbo move, "there was just one thing. David Scott, when he got hurt the other night, there was an ambulance ride and treatment."

"That's something to do with you?"

"Oh, I happened to be at the hospital. Visiting people with milk burns. If you show contrition they don't sue."

Letasha regards her new employee with a wariness she knows will never fade. "What are you saying?"

"Well, some people got the impression that I may have health insurance. And also my name got mentioned. By me. Here's the bill. It is all for David."

"Why are there so many numbers on this?"

"I wasn't happy with either of the second opinions.

We didn't get charged for the tongue depressor and box of Kleenex."

"We?"

"Thank you."

* * *

Frank gives her the next morning off, says his heart could use the respite. It's a wide, clear, fresh fall day and she hoists up the grumbling window to let in some street air that has the vague colour of sand. At the rickety table, she spreads out a forest of paperwork: charities, academic funds, social institutions—all the pots of money big and small scattered all over the country, that added together might make a dance program for kids who can toprock and maybe want more.

Getting into the jargon, this lingo of genteel begging, she's a tad vexed by the tentative knock at the door, one of those knocks that says, 'You're probably out, or can't hear, so I'll try and then leave'.

Not even wondering who it might be, not even pretending to be multiple people, she yanks open the door.

David. With a paper bag. A greasy bag, smelling heavy. "David."

"Hope I didn't disturb you. Thought you'd be at work."

She drags him in. "I am. I mean, I'm filling grant applications. For the theater. We're trying to put together some community programs."

Something here. She pauses.

"Weren't you going to Canada?"

"The others went to Canada. I missed the train. Bear claw?" He jigs it up from the bag like a Sesame Street puppet.

"I got coffee. Just made." She hurries to the kitchenette, so he doesn't see how she's shaking.

While she's gone, he takes a look over the papers. A proposal to do something for gang kids. Dancing in schools, dancing in juvie. Tough gig.

Back she comes with two chipped, mismatched mugs of coffee. Her hair settled back behind her ears, shifting slightly with the breeze from the open window. A Bugs Bunny T-shirt, cake spattered jeans. Her face, in broad daylight, looking exactly her age. Margaret Rudge, looking exactly herself.

He smiles at her. "Coffee and a bear claw."

"So, um," she makes obvious play with her hair, "where you staying now?"

"Handed back the keys on the Airbnb this morning."

"You did?"

"Had to. My bag's in the hall."

"Bring it in. You know," she watches him lever in his skinny black tote, "if Letasha and me get all this together, we're going to need dancers, teachers. Folks who can engage diverse communities."

"What's the pay?" He smiles at her. He so wants to keep smiling at her.

"Oh lousy, totally lousy. Not enough to cover the rent."

"I'll have to make other arrangements then."

"I got," she gestures behind, "this couch. It's really comfortable. And I don't use it, after I go to bed. Got a great view of the TV."

"I couldn't, I mean, I'd need to pay."

"Oh, mop the floor, wash some clothes. A good mopping pays the rent."

He moves naturally toward her. She stands to wait for him. He doesn't see her novelty bunny slippers kicked under the table. He slips on a stray, loppy ear, throwing coffee in Bugs Bunny's face.

"Oh God, I'm sorry," he grabs her arms. "Does that burn?"

"Not really. The stove doesn't heat so well."

She glances down at her wet T-shirt, at Bugs' dripping face.

"Guess I'll have to get changed now. Anyway," she takes his hands, glides him to the bedroom, "anything should dry on a day like this."

Since the 1990s, Mark Wagstaff has published stories in journals and anthologies in the US and UK. In 2016, Mark's story 'Required Fields' was named a Notable Contender in the Bristol Short Story Prize. His story 'Some Secret Space' won the 2013 William Van Wert Fiction Award. In 2012, Mark's story 'Burn Lines' won The New Guard Machigonne Fiction Contest. Mark's second short story collection, also called *Burn Lines*, was published in 2014. Gina Ochsner described the stories in *Burn Lines* as 'lyrically intrepid' while Rick Bass found them 'sweetly ominous.'